No matter how hard she tried to stop the caring from creeping into her heart, she couldn't.

She liked Mitch Dalton. She liked him very much.

"Why do you love pearls?" He studied her, waiting.

"Everyone knows that a pearl starts with a tiny grain of sand, but to me, it's like faith. We are like that grain of sand and it's God's grace that can cloak us and make us shine, if we are humble and faithful enough. In the end, it's a thing of true beauty."

"Yes, it certainly is."

He wasn't looking at the pearl. But at her. Somehow his gaze deepened and there he went, somehow feeling too intimate, as if he could see too much. But how could he look past the layers of defense in which she cloaked herself so carefully?

Books by Jillian Hart

Love Inspired

Heaven Sent #143
*His Hometown Girl #180
A Love Worth Waiting For #203
Heaven Knows #212
*The Sweetest Gift #243
*Heart and Soul #251
*Almost Heaven #260
*Holiday Homecoming #272
*Sweet Blessings #295
For the Twins' Sake #308
*Heaven's Touch #315
*Blessed Vows #327
*A Handful of Heaven #335
*A Soldier for Christmas #367

*The McKaslin Clan

JILLIAN HART

makes her home in Washington State, where she has lived most of her life. When Jillian is not hard at work on her next story, she loves to read, go to lunch with her friends and spend quiet evenings with her family.

Jillian Hart

A Soldier For Christmas

Steeple
Hill®

Published by Steeple Hill Books™

STEEPLE HILL BOOKS

Steeple
Hill®

ISBN-13: 978-0-373-87397-5
ISBN-10:   0-373-87397-2

A SOLDIER FOR CHRISTMAS

Copyright © 2006 by Jill Strickler

www.SteepleHill.com

Printed in U.S.A.

I wait for the Lord, my soul waits,
and in His word I put my hope.
—*Psalms* 130:5

To Frank Heidt. Thanks for taking the time
to answer my questions about Force Recon,
I'll keep your family in prayer, always.

Chapter One

Kelly Logan closed the textbook with a huff and blinked hard to bring the Christian bookstore where she worked into focus.

Math. It was *so* not fair that she, a twenty-four-year-old college student, had to take the required course so she could graduate. She intentionally hadn't thought about quadratic equations since high school, which was six years ago. Hello? Who would want to have to think about this stuff? Unfortunately, she was paying good tuition money to have to think about this stuff. She rubbed her forehead in the hopes that her equation-induced headache would go away.

No such luck. Pain pounded against her temples as though someone was inside her skull, beating her with a mallet. Lovely. She'd been studying algebra for thirty minutes in the quiet lull of a Friday afternoon. Thirty minutes was all it took for her neurotransmitters to quit working in protest. Not that she blamed them. Definitely time for a study break before her head imploded. She leaned a little to the left over the counter to check on the store's only customer, busily browsing in the devotionals display. "Do you need any help, Opal?"

"Any more of your help and I'll break my budget, honey." Elderly Mrs. Opal Finch wandered away from the decorated table with a small book in hand. "I got this one. The one you recommended. I see one of your bosses put up a written recommendation on it, too."

"Katherine has exquisite taste."

Opal slipped the book onto the counter. "Since when have you two steered me wrong? It's such a pretty cover, I couldn't resist."

"Neither could I. I bought it today—payday." Kelly gestured toward the identical small pink book next to her textbooks before she rang up the sale. "I already took a peek at it. The first day's devotion is awesome."

"Wonderful. Are you going to want to see my identification? That new girl did last time I was here."

"Nope, I know your account number by heart."

"That's not what I meant." Opal's merry green eyes sparkled with amusement. "So you can verify my senior citizen discount! It's a hoot, that's what it is, questioning my age. Oh my, it's good for the soul."

"You look eighty-three years young to me," Kelly

assured the lovely octogenarian as she scribbled down the purchase on an in-house charge slip.

"Bless you, dear, I surely appreciate that. And I don't need a bag, sweetie. Conservation, you know." She opened her wide paisley-patterned purse, hanging by sturdy straps from her forearm.

Kelly leaned over the counter to slip the book and receipt into the cavernous purse. "Thanks for coming by. You stop in and tell me how you like the devotional, okay?"

"I most certainly will." Opal snapped her purse shut, her smile beaming and her spirit shining through. "Don't study too hard. An education is important, but don't you forget. There are greater blessings in this life."

In yours, yes. Kelly filed the in-house copy of the charge slip in the till and held back the shadows in her heart. She feared that a happy family may not have been in God's plan for her. Sometimes it was hard to accept, to see the reason why she'd been given the parents she had.

Some days it was all she could do to have faith.

"Kelly, dear," Opal called over her shoulder on the way to the door. "Be sure and tell Katherine goodbye for me. That girl works too much!"

"I'd tell her that, but she won't listen."

The bell over the front door chimed cheerfully as it swung open with a force hard enough to keep the bell tinkling a few extra times.

"Let me hold the door for you, ma'am." A man's rugged baritone sounded as warm as the intense August sunshine, and the bell jingled again as he stepped aside, holding the door wide as Opal passed through.

Something puzzled her. His voice. There was something about it. Kelly couldn't see him well because of the glare of bright sunlight slanting through the open window blinds lining the front of the store.

All she saw of the newcomer was his silhouette cutting through the strong lemony rays of the western sun. It was a silhouette cut so fine, everything within her stilled, awestruck by the iron-strong impression of his wide-shouldered outline.

"Why, thank you, sir," Opal's genteel alto rang with admiration. "You're a fine gentleman."

"You have a nice afternoon, ma'am." He stepped out of the touch of the light. His shadowed form became substance—a fit, capable soldier dressed in military camouflage, who looked as if he'd just walked off the front page of the newspaper and into the bookstore.

Wow. Definitely, one of the good guys.

"Good afternoon." The soldier removed his hat, the floppy brimmed kind that was camouflage, too, revealing his thick, short jet-black hair. He nodded crisply in her direction.

"Uh. G-good afternoon." Was that really her voice? It sounded as if she had peanut butter stuck in her throat. Totally embarrassing. "Do you need any help?"

"I might. I'll let you know." He stood too far away for her to see the color of his eyes accurately, but his gaze was direct and commanding.

And familiar. There *was* something about him. It wasn't uncommon for soldiers to find their way in here, down from the army base up north.

Could he be a repeat customer? She considered him more carefully. No, she sure didn't think he'd been in before. His face was more rugged than handsome, masculine and distinctive with piercing hazel eyes, a sharp blade of a nose and square granite jaw.

Kelly, you're gawking at the guy. Again, a little embarrassing, so she went in search through her backpack instead. Her aspirin bottle was in there somewhere—

"Hey, I know you. You're Kelly, right? Kelly Logan?" The handsome warrior grinned at her, slow and wide, showing straight, even white teeth. Twin dimples cut into lean, sun-browned cheeks. "South Valley High. You don't remember me, do you?"

Then she recognized the little upward crick in the corner of his mouth, making the left side of his smile higher than the right. Like a video on rewind, time reeled backward and she saw the remembered image of a younger, rangy teenage boy.

"Mitch? From sophomore math class. No, it can't be—" Like a cold spray from the leading edge of an avalanche, she felt the slap and the cold. The past rolled over her, and she deliberately shut out the painful blast and held onto the memories of the man standing before her. The shy honors student who'd let her, the new girl, check her homework answers against his for the entire spring quarter.

"Yep, it's me." A very mature Mitch Dalton strode toward her with a leader's confidence. "How are you?"

"Good." A sweet pang kicked to life in her chest. She remembered the girl she used to be. A girl who had stubbornly clung to the misguided hope that her life would be filled with love—one day. Who had still believed in dreaming. "You have changed in a major way."

"Only on the outside. I'm still a shy nerd down deep."

"You don't look it." She glanced at the pile of text-books on the counter. She, on the other hand, was still a shy bookish girl—and looked it.

"You haven't changed much." Mitch halted at the edge of the counter, all six feet plus of solid muscle, towering over her. "I would have known you anywhere."

"Why? Because—wait, don't answer that." She saw the girl she'd been, so lost, so alone, in and out of foster care and relatives' homes. She belonged nowhere, and that had been a brand she'd felt as clearly as if it had been in neon, flashing on her forehead. She still did.

Forget the past. Life was easier to manage when she looked forward and not back.

Mitch jammed his big hands on his hips, and the pose merely emphasized his size and strength. "It's been a long time since we sat in Mr. Metzer's advanced algebra class."

"Math. You had to go and remind me of that particular torture. I was lost until you took pity on me and gave me a little help. I wouldn't have passed Algebra Two without you."

"Math's not so bad. I'm planning on getting a math degree after I get out next summer."

"Out of the army?"

"Please. I'm a marine."

"I should have known. The distinctive camouflage outfit gives it away. Not."

His left eyebrow quirked as he glanced down at his uniform and then at his name on his pocket—M. Dalton. "Did you really remember me, or did you just read the tag?"

"You were too far away when you walked in. So, this is what you've been doing since high school?"

"Yep. Being a soldier keeps me busy and out of trouble."

Kelly wasn't fooled. His hazel eyes sparkled with hints of green and gold, and humor drew fine character lines around his mouth. He didn't look as if he caused trouble. No, he looked as if he stopped trouble when it happened. "Are you stationed up north?"

"It's only temporary. I'm here for more training.

Then it's back to California, and the desert after that. They keep me pretty busy."

"The desert, as in the Middle East? Like, in combat?"

"That's what soldiers do." His smile faded. He watched her with a serious, unblinking gaze, as if he wanted to change subjects. "How's Joe doing?"

"J-Joe." She froze in shock. Didn't Mitch know what had happened? Her chest clogged tight, as if she were buried under a mountain of snow. She wanted to be anywhere, anywhere but here. Talking about anything, anyone.

It felt as if an eternity had passed, but it had to be only the space between one breath and the next.

Silent, Mitch loomed over her, the surface of the wooden counter standing between them wide as the Grand Canyon. The late-afternoon sun sheened on the polished counter, or maybe it was the pain in her eyes that made it seem so bright. Looking through that glare and up into Mitch's face was tough. It was tougher still to try to talk about her broken dreams. They were too personal.

She'd stopped trusting anyone with those vulnerable places within her when she'd buried Joe.

And that's the way she still wanted it.

She slipped her left hand into her jeans pocket so he wouldn't see that there was no ring. She could not bring herself to answer him as the seconds stretched out longer and longer and she looked down at the counter, too numb to think of anything to say, even to change the subject.

The truth of the past remained, unyielding and something she could not go back and change. There were a lot of things in her life she would have wanted to be different. A man as forthright and strong as Mitch Dalton wouldn't understand that. Not at all.

The phone jingled, like a sign from above to move on and let go. She had a reason to step away from the tough marine watching her, as if he could see right into her.

"Excuse me," she said to him and turned away to snatch the phone from the cradle. "Corner Christian Books. How can I help you? Oh, hello, Mrs. Brisbane."

Mitch retreated from the counter, captivated by Kelly's warm, sweet voice. It was still the same.

She was not—quiet, yes, sweet, yes, but wounded. So, what had happened?

Years ago, the first time he'd come home on a much-deserved quick break from his Force Recon training, he'd gotten up the courage to ask his mom first about any hometown news. And then about Kelly in particular.

She's marrying that McKaslin boy she's been dating, Mom had said.

Married. That word had struck him like a bullet against a flak jacket and he'd hidden his disappointment. That had been the last time he'd asked about Kelly Logan.

She wasn't married now, whatever had happened. As he sank into the rows of books, he cast another glance in Kelly's direction. Her gentle tone continued. Clearly she knew and liked the customer who'd called. But this didn't interest him so much as what he could read by simply looking at her. The way she held herself so tightly and defensively, as if she were protecting the deepest places in her heart. The way her smile didn't reach her pretty blue eyes. Sadness clung to the corners of her soft mouth and made her wide almond-shaped eyes look too big in her fragile heart-shaped face.

How much of that sadness had he made worse by putting his foot in his mouth? Troubled, he turned his back, determined to leave thoughts of the woman behind, but they followed him through the long shelves of Bibles and into the Christian fiction rows. He still reeled from the raw pain he'd recognized in Kelly's eyes.

He'd been so wrapped up in his life, in his demanding job and nearly constant deployments, that he'd almost forgotten that heartbreak and tragedy happened off the battlefield, too.

Pain. He hated that she'd been hurt. He hated that he'd been the one to bring up the past. He should have looked at her hand first, the ringless left hand she'd been trying to hide from him, before he'd said anything. Something had happened to her, something painful, and he was sorry about that.

Wasn't pain the result of relationships? He saw it all the time. Marriages failed all around him, it happened to his friends, his team members, marines he barely knew and to his commanding officers.

Between the betrayal when a spouse broke wedding vows or changed into a different person, and the grief when love ended, he didn't know how anyone could give their hearts at all, ever, knowing the risks. Knowing the pain.

That was why he kept clear of relationships. Not only did he not have much free time to get to know a woman, but he wondered how anyone knew when it was the real thing—the kind of love that lasted, the kind his parents had—or the kind of relationship that ended with devastation.

Either way, it was a lot more risk than he'd felt comfortable with.

So, why was he searching for a view of Kelly? From where he stood, the solid wooden bookshelves blocked the front counter, so he stepped a little to his left until he could see her reflected in the glass like a mirror. Perfect.

He wanted to say it was guilt, of bringing up something painful that had happened with Joe, that made him notice the way the soft fluff of her golden bangs covered her forehead and framed her big, wide eyes. And how the curve of her cheek and jaw looked as smooth as rose petals. Her hair curled past her jawline and fell against the graceful line of her neck to curl against the lace of her blouse's collar.

But that wasn't the truth. Guilt wasn't why he was noticing her. Concern wasn't the only reason he couldn't seem to tear his gaze away. He was interested. He was stationed here for a short stint, that was all, and he wasn't looking for anything serious— that was a scary thought.

No, he wasn't ready for that. He didn't have time for that. He wasn't a teenaged kid anymore with an innocent crush, and by the look of things, Kelly'd had her heart broken. She probably wasn't looking, either.

He'd come here to find a gift—nothing more— and he'd be smart to get to it. That was the sensible thing to do. He wandered back to the aisle of Bibles, determined to keep his attention focused squarely on his difficult mission: finding a suitable birthday gift.

The rustle of her movements jerked his attention back to her. He was at the end of the row, giving him a perfect view of Kelly. She'd hung up the phone and was circling around the edge of the long front counter. She was keeping her eyes low and intentionally not looking his way, but he kept observing her as he went on with his browsing.

He couldn't say why he watched her as she padded to the far edge of the store. Or why he noticed how elegant she looked in a simple pink cotton blouse and slim khaki pants. It was a mystery. He wanted to attribute it to his training—the marines had trained him well and paid him to observe, but that wasn't it at all. Not truthfully.

He couldn't say why, but he listened to the whisper of her movements and kept listening…even after she'd disappeared from his sight.

Chapter Two

Was it her imagination, or was he watching her?

Kelly slipped the inspirational romance from its spot on the shelf. Her gaze shot between the open book bay to watch the hunky soldier's broad back, which was all she could see of him. Mitch stood with his feet braced apart, browsing through the devotionals display midway across the store.

No, he's not even looking my way, she thought, shaking her head and hurrying back to the cash desk. Besides, he seemed totally absorbed in his browsing as he set down one book and reached for another. He was the only customer in the store, and if he wasn't noticing her, then no one was.

Okay, so she was nuts, but she still felt...*watched*. She remembered the impact of his gaze, and how tangible it had felt. She kept a careful eye on him as she returned to the front.

Although he didn't lift his head or turn in her direction, she felt monitored the entire time it took for her to write Edith Brisbane's name on a slip of paper, rubber-band it to the spine of the book and slip it onto the hold shelf.

I know what the problem is, she realized in the middle of shaking an aspirin tablet onto her palm. *She* was the one noticing *him*.

Who could blame her? He cut a fine figure in his rugged military uniform, and back in high school she'd always had a secret crush on him. He'd always been a truly nice boy. It looked as if time had only improved him.

As she chased the aspirin down with a few swallows from a small bottle of orange soda, her gaze automatically zoomed across the floor to him. Head bent, he had moved on to amble through the gift section of the store, his attention planted firmly on the rows of porcelain jewelry boxes in front of him. There were two inspirational suspense books tucked in one big hand.

When she looked at him, she could hear his gravelly voice asking again, How's Joe doing?

It wasn't his fault, Mitch obviously didn't know what had happened. But that didn't make the raw places within her heart hurt any less.

She was no longer a girl who could dream.

She climbed back onto her stool and debated tackling more of her homework, but she wasn't in the mood to face her math book. She knew that if she sat here trying to solve for x, her attention would just keep drifting over to the impressive warrior. To the past.

What good could come from that?

"Hey, Kelly." Her boss's solemn baritone cut through her thoughts, spinning her around to face him. Spence McKaslin pushed open the door on the other side of the hold shelf. He emerged from the fluorescent glare of his office, looking gruff, the way he always did when he worked on the accounts. "I'll be in the back going through the new order. Katherine's still out, so if it gets busy, buzz me."

"Sure, but it's been really quiet. Do you want me to start restocking or something?"

"No, we're all caught up. Just watch the front until your dinner break. Study while you can. It could get busy later."

"It never gets busy on a Friday night."

"Don't argue with me, I'm the boss." He gave her an extra-hard glare on his way to the drawers beneath the till, but he didn't fool her.

Spence was strong and stoic and tough, but also one of the kindest men she'd ever met. Her opinion of him had been pretty high ever since he'd hired her, which had saved her from losing her apartment when she'd been laid off from her previous job. Spence would have been her cousin, had things worked out differently with Joe.

A lot of things would have been different if she'd been able to marry Joe.

Feeling as if she'd been sucker-punched, she tried hard not to let the pain show. She didn't know how something so powerful would ever go away, but she did her best to tuck her grief down deep inside. Her gaze strayed to where Mitch still browsed, looking like everything good and noble and strong in the world.

But she also saw memories. And she wanted nothing to do with the past.

Spence grabbed the key ring from its place under the counter and studied her in the assessing way of a good big brother. "Did you manage to fit in lunch today?"

"Well, I ate a granola bar while I was stuck in traffic in the big parking lot on campus."

"I knew it. Take your dinner break at five, and I'll go when you get back," he ordered over his shoulder, already marching away.

Mitch watched the older man pass by the gift section and disappear through a door in the back. It was less than an hour before her dinner break. Interesting. He couldn't say why, but he felt out of his element. And it wasn't because he was in a store full of flowery knickknacks and breakables.

A plan hatched in the back of his mind, and it had nothing to do with his shopping mission.

Kelly remained in his peripheral vision. She made a lovely picture, sitting straight-backed with her head bowed over a book. The math text was still in the stack, so she must be working on another subject.

Absorbed in her reading, she tucked a strand of rich honey-blond hair behind her ear, revealing a small pearl earring and her bare left hand.

While he was at home creeping through enemy territory in the rugged mountains of Afghanistan or the deserts of the Middle East, his extensive training did not include what he was about to do.

He kept her in his line of sight as he approached the register. The light from the window seemed to find her and grace her with a golden glow. She kept her head bowed over her book as he approached, but her shoulders stiffened with tension. Telling. But he continued his approach, taking in other details. The soda bottle, her nearly worn-out leather watchband, the pink barrette in her hair that matched the tiny flowers on her blouse. The two sociology textbooks stacked neatly at her left elbow.

He wondered about her life. Did she like being a college student? Did she live on campus in a dorm room or in a nearby apartment? Alone, or with a roommate?

When she looked up from her reading, her smile was cordial but he didn't mistake the sadness, like a shadow, in her dark-blue eyes. He felt a tug of sympathy from his heart. "You look pretty busy," he noted, easing the books onto the counter by her register.

"It's the life of a college student. I have a test on Monday." As she leaned to scan the books, her hair bounced across the side of her face, leaving only a small sliver of her profile visible. "Did you find what you were looking for?"

"I found more." He wasn't talking about the books.

"I do that all the time." Her gaze didn't meet his and her polite smile was too brief. She turned her attention to the cash register. All business.

Okay, he got the signal, but he didn't let it deter him. "How long 'til you get your degree?"

"After this summer, I have two semesters left." She paused to study the cash register and searched for a key.

"It's gotta be slow going, working your way through."

"It's taking twice as long, but at least I don't have a major loan to pay back when I'm done."

"That's one perk of enlisting. My college will be paid for."

At least he wasn't mentioning the past or Joe again, Kelly thought thankfully as she totaled the sale. Her chest was still clogged tight, like the fallout of an avalanche still pressing her down. "Twenty-one ninety-three, please."

Mitch held out his credit card.

When her fingertips caught the other end, she felt a flash, like a shock of static electricity in the air. The sunlight changed to a bright piercing white. The floor rocked beneath her feet. It lasted only for a second. Then the earth steadied, the sunlight turned golden and there was Mitch, unmoved, looking calm and as cool as steel.

That was *so* not a sign from heaven. Just the pieces of what remained of her dreams, longing, in the way faint embers from a fire's flame could glow briefly to life when exposed to air. Her fingers trembled as she swiped his card and plunked it back onto the polished counter between them.

If there was a way to breathe life back into her dreams, she would ask the Lord to show her how. But she didn't bother. Some things really were impossible. "I still can't believe you're a soldier. What happened to your pocket protector?"

"No place for it on this uniform. I love what I do."

"What exactly do you do?"

"Well, I started out at oh-six-hundred with a ten click—kilometer—run in full gear and spent the day mountain climbing to five thousand feet."

"You get paid to climb mountains?"

"That's not all. I get to do things like scuba dive, parachute, drive around in Humvees and play with explosives." He said it all as if it was no big deal, just in a humble day's work. "Keeps me out of trouble."

"Seems like that would get you *into* trouble."

"Nothing I can't handle."

Wow, Kelly thought, as she bagged the books. He's grown up into quite a man. "See, my day is a piece of cake by comparison."

"Except for the math."

"Oh, you *had* to mention that again. I was trying to forget for a while." She hadn't laughed out loud in a long time. "Where you get paid to do things that you think are fun, I pay out good tuition money to be tortured by algebra."

"I'll be in your boat in eighteen months."

"That's right. That math degree you're going to get." The machine spat out the charge receipt and she held the two-part paper steady while it printed. How her heart ached as those embers of old dreams struggled for life. She tore off the printed receipt and slid it across the counter. "I need your autograph, and then you're free to go, soldier."

"*Free's* a relative term." He grabbed a pen from the cup by the register. "My time's pretty regimented."

"I bet it is. Are you headed back to your base?"

"In a few hours. I'm free until then." He scrawled his signature at the bottom of the slip.

Too bad she'd given up on dreams. She didn't know if she felt relief or regret.

"I hope you enjoy your books." She slipped his receipt into the bag and presented it to him. "I'm glad to see you're doing so well. I wish you luck, Mitch."

"You're letting me go, just like that?"

"Well, what else am I supposed to do? Generally we let customers leave our store. We seldom hold them hostage."

"I'm not talking about other customers. I'm talking about me. We could renew our friendship."

"We were never really friends, you know."

What did that leave him with? Renewing his secret crush on her? He took his bag, but the last thing he wanted to do was leave. She was still the nicest girl he'd ever laid eyes on. He could use a little nice in his world. It wasn't something he saw much of.

"We could be friends now," he suggested with his best grin.

"But you said you were headed back to California." Sweetly, she studied him through her long lashes.

A mass of emotions struck him like shrapnel to his chest. Emotions weren't his realm of expertise, but he felt strong with a fierce steely need he'd never felt before—to protect her, to make her smile, to make her every sadness go away.

Not really in his comfort zone, but a crush was a crush. What was a guy to do?

He tried again. "I'm not leaving for a while. We could still be friends."

"I have enough friends." Her eyebrow crooked up in a challenge.

So, she was giving him a hard time on purpose. "You get a dinner break, right?"

"Now and then they loosen the chains and let me out for a bit." Kelly folded her arms in front of her, considering him.

"You get a dinner break, and I'm hungry for dinner. It's a coincidence."

Kelly couldn't believe how he was just watching her with those intense, commanding hazel eyes of his, so wise and perceptive. She felt the impact as if he could see directly into her. "You're asking me out, aren't you?"

"No, not out. No. Of course not." He held up his free hand, as if he were innocent. Completely guilt-free.

"That's good, because I don't date anymore. I'm sorry."

"That's okay, because I'm not looking for a date. I was asking you to help me out."

"As if a big strong soldier like you needs any help at all?"

"Sure. I need a favor. I'm a lonely marine."

"A lonely marine?" Oh, she was *so* not fooled.

"Sure. It's only dinner." Amusement quirked the left side of his mouth. "C'mon, you gotta eat."

"True, but you probably have better things to do on a Friday evening."

"I can't think of one."

It's gotta be the uniform, she told herself as she assessed him carefully. "They must not let you out much if you think sharing my dinner break is your best option."

"What can I say? I could use a friend. How about it?"

Kelly's heart twisted hard. There was no mistaking the sincerity in his steady gaze. He meant those words. How could she say no? She knew a thing or two about wanting a friend. "You've got a deal."

"Excellent. How do you like your hamburger?"

"With cheese and mayo, no onions and tomatoes."

"I'll be back in an hour. Thanks, Kelly. I'm glad I ran into you."

"I'm glad, too."

He was military-strong *and* nice. What a combo. She couldn't help liking him. Who wouldn't?

She watched him stride away, cutting through the long rays of sunlight and disappearing into the glare. She couldn't help the little sigh that escaped her. The bell jingled and the door swished shut and he was gone.

The dying embers in her heart ached. Be careful, she warned herself, holding on tight to her common sense. A man like Mitch could make her want to believe. And it was the wanting that got her into trouble every time—the longing to belong, to be loved, to know that soft comfort of a loving marriage and family.

"Hey, who was that?" Back from her run to the bank, Katherine, Spence's sister, swished behind the counter. "He looked like a very nice, very solid, very fine young man."

"Oh, that was just a customer."

"No, he was trying to ask you out. I happened to overhear. Accidentally, of course." Katherine leaned against her closed office door, looking as if she'd just received the best news.

That was Katherine. Always wishing for happy endings for other people. "It's not how it looks. We're just friends."

"Right, well, that's the best way to start out. You never know what will develop from there. I'm saying prayers for you. No one deserves a happy ending more than you."

"There are no such things as happy endings." Kelly knew that for an absolute fact. "This isn't a fairy tale. He's only in town for a little while."

"You just never know what the Lord has in store for you. It wasn't fair what happened with Joe."

She had to go and mention it. Kelly swallowed hard, wrestling down painful memories—the weight of them heavy on her heart, along with too many regrets. Too many failures. "Life is like that. It's not fair."

"No, but in the end, good things happen to good people. I believe that." Katherine breezed into her office, sure of her view of the world.

Kelly didn't have the heart to believe. She could not let herself dream. Not even the tiniest of wishes. She was no longer a girl who believed in fairy tales, but a grown woman who kept her feet on the ground.

She had no faith left for dreaming.

Chapter Three

❧

"I think it's gonna be a quiet Friday night." Spence emerged from one of the fiction aisles with a book in hand. "How's the studying coming?"

"I'm less confused, I think. I haven't taken math since high school and I've forgotten just about everything but the basics."

"That's why I use a calculator." Spence nodded toward the front windows. "The soldier who was in here earlier? He's back."

"He is?" It took all her effort to sound unaffected. She turned slowly toward the front, as if she hadn't been of two minds about their upcoming dinner. She squinted through the harsh sunshine that haloed the wide-shouldered man.

She recognized the silhouette striding away from a dusty Jeep, carrying a big take-out bag and a cardboard drink carrier in one hand. The light gave him a golden glow, and he was all might and strength and integrity. She remembered what he'd said about needing a friend. It had to be a lonely life he'd chosen.

Spence cleared his throat. "I'm glad you're dating again."

Heat crept up her face. She busily set the alarm on her watch, so she wouldn't go over her allotted break time. "It isn't like that, Spence. Really."

"Okay." Like Katherine, he didn't sound as if he believed her. "Go ahead. Have a nice time."

It was Mitch. How could she not have a nice visit? As he strode her way, she beat him to the door. His welcoming smile was lopsided and friendly—definitely a smile that could make a girl dream. "I'm free for half an hour."

"I'm glad they loosened the chains." His shadow fell across her, covering her completely. "Wanna eat across the street? I saw a couple of tables and benches. Okay?"

"Sure. I eat over there all the time."

Walking at his side, she realized that he was bigger and taller than she had thought. He was a big powerful bear of a guy, his field boots thudding against the pavement. She felt safe with him. Comfortable. "Isn't Montana a little landlocked for a marine?"

"It would be, if I worked on a ship. That would be navy."

"But you're training at the army base?"

"I'm doing some advanced mountaineering. They train their Rangers there, and they're letting my platoon climb around on their rocks."

"Advanced mountaineering. That sounds serious."

"We're doing tactical stuff while we're climbing," he explained with a shrug.

"You must be pretty good."

"I haven't fallen yet."

She stopped at his side, at the curb, waiting for the few cars and trucks to pass. "What exactly do you do in the marines?"

"I'm like a scout. It's clear," he said, referring to the traffic and, as he stepped off the curb, laid his free hand on her shoulder. Not exactly guiding her, as much as guarding.

Kelly shivered down to her soul. Nice. Very nice. What girl wouldn't appreciate a soldier's protective presence? They stepped up on the curb together on the other side of the road, and his hand fell away. The world felt a little lonelier.

"How about that table?" She nodded toward the closest picnic table in the park, which was well shaded beneath a pair of broad-leafed maples.

"That'll work," he agreed amicably.

It was hard to keep pace with him as they made their way across the lush, clipped grass. He didn't walk so much as he power walked, even though he was obviously shortening his long-legged pace for her. She had to hurry to keep up with him as he crossed the grass. "How long are you going to be in Montana?"

"I've been here three weeks. I've got five more to go." He set the drinks and food on the table, then pulled out the bench for her. "That means I'll be outta here mid-September."

"And then back to California?"

"Like I said, they keep me busy." Mitch could only nod. He waited while she settled onto the bench, and the breeze brought a faint scent of her vanilla shampoo. The warmth in his chest changed to something sweeter.

She watched him with gentle blue eyes. "I didn't know marines climbed mountains."

"We climb whatever we're ordered to climb." He freed a large cup from the carrier. "I brought orange soda or root beer. The lady picks first."

"I love orange soda. Good guess."

He didn't mention that he'd noticed the pop bottle she'd had on the store counter beside her schoolbooks. He set the cup beside her. Had she figured out that this was a date yet?

"Cheeseburger, as ordered." He handed out the chow. "Do you want to say grace or will you let me?"

"Go for it." She folded her hands, so sincere.

He brimmed with a strange tenderness as he bowed his head together with hers. "Dear Father, thank you for watching over us today. Please bless this food and our renewed friendship. Amen."

"Amen." A renewed friendship, huh? Kelly unclasped her hands and unwrapped her burger. At least he wasn't trying to make this a date. "Why the marines?"

"That's easy." He dug a few ketchup containers out of the bottom of the bag and as the wind caught the empty sack, he anchored it. "My life has a purpose. I make a difference."

"That matters to you." She took a long look at him. "Making a difference matters to me, too."

"When I was a kid, watching the news coverage of Desert Storm, I was blown away by this segment they did on the marines. They were these powerful men with weapons, and they were taking care of refugees from the fighting. One of the refugees said how amazed he was by these big men. They looked fearsome, but they were also kind."

That pretty much summed it up for her. Kelly blinked and tried to act as if his words hadn't sunk into her heart. He'd grown up and grown well. She only had to look into his clear, expressive eyes to know that he was a very fine man.

Mitch took a big bite of his burger and leaned closer to dig a handful of fries out of the container. "Then it hit me, just how great that was in this world. To be a warrior fierce enough to protect and defend, to stand for what is right. That's honor, in my opinion. And that's how I serve. I do my very best every day."

What on earth did she say to that? She seemed frozen in place. She wasn't breathing. It seemed as if her heart had stopped beating. His gaze met hers, and the honest force of it left her even more paralyzed. The magnitude of his gaze bored into hers like a touch, and she felt the stir of it in her soul, a place where she let no one in. How had he gotten past her defenses?

He grabbed more fries. "How about you?"

"M-me?"

"Sure. Why social work?"

"I didn't tell you that."

"I noticed your textbooks. Are you getting your degree in sociology and a masters in social work?"

"That's the plan. I want to help children. There's a lot of need out there."

"There is." His voice deepened with understanding. There was something about a powerful man who radiated more than just might, but heart, too. "I remember back in high school that you were on your own a lot."

Keep the pain out of your words, she reminded herself. She wasn't willing to confess about the loneliness and the fears of a child growing up the way she did. "I know I can help kids who are in a similar situation. I want to make a difference."

"I'm sure you can." He studied her, his hazel eyes intensified. It was as if he could see the places within her that no one could. "You were in foster care. Is that right?"

"On and off, depending on whether or not my mom was in jail for drugs or if my aunt's bipolar disorder was under control." She forced her gaze from his, breaking contact, but it was too late. She already felt so revealed. "I was lucky. I made it through all right. A lot of kids aren't so fortunate."

"You've done very well for yourself."

"Not by myself."

"By the grace of God?" Mitch waited as Kelly stared toward the far end of the park. There was nothing there, no people to watch, no traffic, nothing but a row of shrubs shivering slightly in the balmy evening breezes. He knew it wasn't the foliage she saw, but the past.

He didn't take for granted one second of his life, especially his childhood with two loving parents in a middle-class suburb. It was a start in life for which he was thankful. "About six years ago, I was training at Coronado when I got the word my dad had had a heart attack. I made it home in time to see him before he went into surgery. I think the good Lord was reminding my family just how lucky we are. We take nothing for granted, not anymore."

"Wise move."

He washed his emotions down with the ice-cold soda. "I've seen enough of the world to know that I wouldn't be who I am without them. It's a blessing to have parents like mine. Remember that favor I mentioned back in the store?"

She dragged a pair of fries through the ketchup container. "I thought this *dinner* was the favor."

"Nope, this is my apology. For sticking my foot in my mouth and bringing up a subject that hurt you."

"You couldn't have known. It's all right." She froze for a moment, and sadness flashed in her eyes again. "What's this favor?"

"I've been trying to find a gift for my mom. No luck. I'm clueless."

"You don't look clueless. And you can't be serious. You look around, you find things and you buy them. It's called shopping. That's how you find a gift. Our store is full of wonderful gifts. Why didn't you say something when you were in before?"

"I wanted to get a look at the jewelry store down the street first."

"Jewelry is always good. We have some lovely gold crosses."

"That's what I got her last Christmas. She has everything else, a mother's ring, more lockets than she can count. A charm bracelet so full of charms there's no room for more. I need help."

"You certainly need something." He was way too charming for her own good, Kelly decided. And she had a hard time saying no to a worthy cause. "When do you need this gift?"

"Her birthday dinner is Sunday night."

"I should have known. A last-minute gift."

"Last minute? What do you mean?" He feigned mock insult. "This is Friday. I have two more days."

Why wasn't she surprised? Kelly took the last bite of her burger. "Okay, what are your parameters?"

"Something unique. Personal. It has to be fairly inexpensive. I'm thinking around a hundred dollars."

"That's not so inexpensive. Have you tried the mall?"

"You're kidding, right? I avoid those at all costs."

"Why is that?"

"No amount of military training can prepare a guy for the conditions that await him in a mall. I'm mall-phobic."

She seriously doubted that. She couldn't imagine Mitch being afraid of anything. "Mall-phobia. I *think* I read about that in my abnormal psychology class."

"Funny. So, you'll help me?"

"It's the least I can do for a friend." *Friend* being the operative word. The beep of her alarm made her jump. Had that much time gone by already? "I've got to go."

"Duty calls."

"Exactly. Did you want to come with me? We can go through the sales books together."

"No time." Disappointment settled like lead inside him. "I've got to be back by twenty hundred hours, and I've got over a two-hour drive ahead of me."

Was it his imagination, or did she look disappointed? Good. Now was the time to set up date number two. "I'm coming back to town on Sunday. How about the two of us get together and put in some serious shopping time?"

"Sunday, then." She folded her empty burger wrapper neatly.

He held the food sack open for her, waiting to toss in his wrapper, crumpled into a ball, after hers. "Where do you want me to pick you up?"

She grabbed one last fry from the tub before she twisted off the bench, graceful and lovely. She backed away, studying him through her long lashes with those big stormy-blue eyes. "The Gray Stone Church on the corner of Glenrose and Cherry Lane. Meet me there. Ten o'clock sharp."

"Meet you there? No, I should pick you up."

"It's not a date, remember?"

Have it your way, pretty lady. He watched her jog away, her hair brushing the back of her shoulders and swinging in time with her gait.

Mitch could only stare, unable to move, waiting as she crossed the street. She was like a vision, awash with light. He remained vigilant until she reached the storefront and disappeared inside.

You're heading to Afghanistan in six weeks, he thought, hardly noticing the crinkling sound the food sacks made when he bunched them and tossed them into the garbage can. What he did was dangerous. He'd learned the value of starting each day without regrets.

If he didn't make the most of this second chance to get to know Kelly, wherever that path might lead, he'd regret it. Six months from now, he'd be shivering on some rock in the border mountains of Afghanistan or belly down on a dune in the Middle East, and he didn't want to be wondering *what if*.

It wasn't only exhaustion weighing her down as she climbed the flight of steps to her apartment. Not the late hour or the dark shadows that fell from the whispering poplars. She felt as if the past clung to her with a tenacious grip tonight, like the stars to the black velvet sky.

Kelly sorted through her key ring as she climbed the outside stairs that brought her to her third-story landing.

In the end, good things happen to good people. I believe that. Katherine's words. They were part of what troubled her tonight and made the shadows so dark, the quiet so deep. Those words haunted her last steps and followed her into the soft pool of illumination from the light over her door. She fitted her key into the deadbolt and turned it with a click. The metallic sound seemed to echo in the chambers of her heart.

Everyone she'd ever depended on had let her down, so it was hard to believe in good things. God never promised that life would be easy or fair. A heart can be broken too much. And she'd learned that every time a heart is broken, it is never the same again.

She withdrew the key and inserted it into the doorknob, turning the knob and shouldering open the door. Her heavy backpack clunked against the door as she stepped through the fall of porch light and into the dark quiet of the foyer.

Mitch had stirred up some of this uneasiness, too. What a great guy. At least he was only interested in a friendship. How could it be anything else, with him leaving for California and beyond?

She could relax and not worry about him leaving—it was a given. She knew what to expect.

The luminous numbers of her stove's clock cast a green glow bright enough to see by as she pushed the door shut behind her, turned the deadbolt and slipped her keys onto the small table between the door and the hall closet. Her pack made a thump when she set it on the floor.

Hot, stifling air greeted her thanks to keeping off the air conditioning. She headed straight for the living room and unlocked the wide window. Cooler air felt heavenly against her overheated skin. She stood for a moment letting the breeze fan over her. Outside the poplars cast dancing shadows from the streetlights and rustled cheerfully. She pressed her hot forehead to the cooler glass, breathed in the fresh night air and let her feelings and thoughts settle.

Mitch. Just thinking of him brought a smile to her face. He was back at his base by now. This was going to be different—interesting, but different—to have him for a friend.

She was actually looking forward to Sunday.

Chapter Four

Mitch scanned the light-veiled sanctuary, crowded with worshippers and loud with their conversations, searching for Kelly. To find her, he only had to follow the sunshine as it slanted through the glittering panels of stained glass.

Kelly. When he saw her, brushed with golden light and goodness, his heartbeat skipped. The sanctuary, full of light and sound and families getting settled, faded away and only the silence remained. She was sitting in a pew near the middle, her head bowed as if reading.

She hadn't noticed him yet, so he took a moment just to drink in the sight of her. Her honey-gold hair was unbound and framed her heart-shaped face. The lavender summer dress she wore shaped her delicate shoulders and fell in a complimentary sweep to her knees. A book bag slumped on the bench beside her. Matching purple flats hugged her slim feet.

He liked the way she looked, so pure and bright. She made a lovely picture, sitting so straight, with her Bible open on her lap. It wasn't too much of a hardship to look at her. He eased into the row and onto the pew beside her.

She jumped, and her Bible tumbled onto the polished wood bench between them. "Mitch! You snuck up on me!"

"Hey, I'm no sneak."

"Then what do you call that? You didn't make a sound. That's sneaking in my book." Her eyes twinkled like aquamarines.

Enchanted—he was simply enchanted. *And* she looked glad to see him. What was a helpless guy to do? He shrugged. "Sorry. It's habit, I guess. Didn't mean to scare you."

"You are a scary man, Mitch Dalton." Her smile said the opposite as he rescued her fallen Bible from the bench between them. "Do you have a chance to attend a service when you're overseas?"

"Usually a chaplain holds service every Sunday. I attend whenever I'm in camp." He studied the Bible in his hands. It looked like his, treasured and well-read. He handed it over. "This is some church. It beats a tent hands down."

"A tent, huh?" Her fingertips brushed against his, feather-light and brief.

Wow. Her touch stilled his senses. As if from somewhere far away organ music began, and late worshippers hurried to find seats as the minister stepped up to his podium. The congregation rose.

Kelly stood, and somehow he was on his feet beside her. She was so small and feminine at his side. All he knew was that he liked being with her. Not a comfortable thing for the lone wolf he was. But not bad, either.

She went up on tiptoe to tell him something, and he had to lean so she could manage to whisper in his ear. "I'm wearing my shopping shoes. I hope you can keep up with me."

That was funny. Little did she know what he was capable of doing in a single day. "Bring it on, little lady. I can do anything you can do."

"Be careful. I just might drag you to a mall."

"Hey, we had a no-mall agreement."

"I made no promises, soldier."

Kelly felt as light as air. Happy. She'd been working and studying so hard lately, she was glad she'd agreed to spend this time with Mitch. Besides, it was never a bad thing to have a handsome man— er, *friend*—sit beside you at church.

Mitch. She couldn't help noticing he had a very nice singing voice and yet he didn't attract attention to himself. His voice was quiet and his manner solemn. And he stood powerful and tall. Very masculine.

Not that she was wishing.

As she bowed her head for prayer, she caught sight of the Bible passage on the program. The typed words were the last thing she saw as she closed her

eyes and the words from Isaiah emblazoned them-
selves on her eyelids. "Whether you turn to the right
or to the left, your ears will hear a voice behind you
saying, 'This is the way, walk in it.'"

It had also been the exact passage from her
morning devotional. Coincidence? Probably not.

I'm trying, Lord, to follow where You lead.

But she was so adrift. Even with Mitch at her
side. Even in the peace of God's sanctuary with
heaven's light falling all around her.

"Whether you turn to the right or to the left, your
ears will hear a voice behind you saying, 'This is the
way, walk in it.'"

With the minister's message in his heart, Mitch
stayed at Kelly's side as they inched patiently down
the main aisle. Maybe this was a sign he was on the
right path. A new one for him, considering his
wariness of long-term relationships. And a strange
one, because God's plan for him was thousands of
miles away, across an ocean.

Kelly introduced him to the minister, who warmly
thanked him for coming. As they followed the de-
parting worshippers down the front steps and out
into the bright sunshine, he stayed at Kelly's side,
protecting her from any jostling from the crowd.

"Well, soldier, are you ready for your mission? Or
do I leave you to survive shopping as best you can?"
Her smile was as sweet as spun sugar.

He liked it. "I've already confessed that I'm retail-challenged."

"A big tough guy like you? C'mon, soldier up." She winked, and couldn't help laughing. "I expect a marine to be tougher than that."

"I'll survive with a pretty girl like you watching my six."

"Your six? Oh, I get it. Watching your back. You're going to need it where I'm taking you. Peril and danger abound."

"I live for danger."

"That makes two of us." Kelly liked the look of worry crinkling his forehead. She guessed he was only halfway kidding her about having mall-phobia. "At ease, sir. I spent some time thinking of a few good ideas for your mom. And we don't have to set foot inside any mall."

"I'm gonna owe you big-time for this."

"No way. What's a little favor between friends?"

Mitch frowned. He had to set the groundwork for date number three. Something gave him a clue that she wouldn't make it easy for him.

He'd just have to wow her so much, she'd want to go out with him again. Maybe even call it a date next time. A man could hope. "You wanna grab a bite first?"

"I didn't think you soldiers took detours when you were on a mission."

"Right, but I'm gonna need fuel. No way can I shop on an empty stomach. Oh, wait. I get it. You don't date. And you're afraid that eating together twice would make it look like we're dating."

"It *could* look that way, but it's not. Right?"

Was that a shadow of fear he saw in her gentle blue eyes? Why would she be afraid? Then in a blink, it was gone.

He stepped off the curb, looking for traffic, but there were no cars headed their way. He fished his keys from his pocket. "Don't even worry. Friends go out to eat together sometimes."

"I just don't want you to get the wrong idea. I know you'll be leaving in a month or so—"

"Exactly, so don't sweat it. We'll do whatever you want."

"I've got the best shop to show you. I really think you'll find what you want there."

"You mean this could be a one-stop deal?"

"It might even be painless."

She was doing her best to thwart his plans for their date. He was going down in flames. Not good. This had to be about Joe. What had happened? What had he done to her? He hadn't known the guy except as a name back in high school.

Whatever had happened, it had sure made Kelly afraid to try dating again. As he unlocked the passenger door, a mild breeze whispered through the maples overhead and shifted the lemony sunshine over them. In the dappled mix of shadows and light he opened the door and took Kelly's hand to help her up.

She dodged him, as if too independent for such a gesture, but he sensed it was something more as she slipped past him. Her cotton dress gave a whispering rustle, and the vanilla fragrance from her shampoo scented the air between them.

Unaware of how she moved him, she climbed into the passenger seat and settled her book bag on the floor at her feet. She sat there in a swirl of lavender summer cotton and dappled sunlight and sweetness. Feelings came to life within his heart and weren't like anything he'd felt before. They were soft and warm, and as soothing as prayer. Tenderness lit him up from the inside out. He felt every inch of his six-foot-two-inch frame as he closed her door and circled around to his side.

Her smile was calm, her blue eyes bright and friendly. "It's not far from here. If you can pull a U-turn and avoid the traffic jam up the street?"

"Inciting me to break the law, huh?" He winked as he started the engine and belted in. "I'm shocked. A sweet girl like you."

"Ah, the things you don't know about me."

"I'm beginning to get the picture. A hard-working college student who goes to church every Sunday. Yep, you're trouble." He checked the mirrors and the pedestrian traffic before turning sharply out from the curb and down the narrow tree-lined residential street.

Then he saw the sign, allowing U-turns in the wide, turnabout intersection.

"No more trouble than you are, I bet. Sunday service and then dinner at home with your parents."

"Not until six tonight. Until then, I'm a reckless man on the town." A gray tabby cat paraded off the sidewalk about ten yards up the residential street, and he slowed to a stop.

"Yeah, reckless. I see that."

He could feel her gaze like the softest brush against the line of his profile. He'd like to know what she thought about him. Come September he'd be on a bird out of here and he wouldn't be back this way again except for a rare, quick family holiday.

He wanted...he didn't know what he wanted. But he liked being with her.

Once the cat was safely across the street, he hit the gas. A four-way stop was ahead. "Which way?"

"Right. And take the first parking spot you come to."

"It's that easy? I can't believe it." He whipped the Jeep over to the curb and parked. "I just might make it out of this mission without a casualty."

"No casualties, remember? I'm watching your six."

"Then let's do it." He killed the engine and released his seat belt.

Kelly took a deep breath and tried to steady herself, to just breathe. What she couldn't explain was why he'd affected her like this. Why he'd slipped through her defenses as if they were nothing.

She didn't have a clue. He was already out of

the Jeep and slamming the door, moving with an easy, latently powerful bearing around the front of the vehicle.

Why was she watching him? Because it was impossible not to. He looked like everything good in the world, honorable and strong. He made the broken places within her heart feel less cracked. He made her laugh and smile.

It was hard not to like him a little more for being a gentleman as he caught the edge of the door when she opened it with his big powerful hand. Golden flecks twinkled in his eyes as he grinned at her. "This might not be a date, but I'm getting the doors for you anyway."

"You're going to spoil me, and then where will I be?"

"You'll be treated the way you deserve." He held out his big hand, palm up and waiting.

She hesitated. He was simply being a gentleman, nothing more, but that's what scared her. There was danger in taking even the first tiny step in leaning on anyone. When you started leaning, you started hoping.

And in the hoping, dreaming.

The pieces of her broken heart ached like shattered bone. Friendship was one thing, but she could get out of the Jeep on her own, thank you very much.

As she tipped off the edge of the seat, his hand shot out, caught her forearm, the tricky guy. His grip was iron-strong and commanding. The warmth of his touch, and the strength of it, rocked through her.

Instead of feeling afraid, peace ebbed into her heart. Even into the broken places.

Her feet hit the concrete sidewalk, jarring her back into reality. Mitch let go, and shut the door with a thump. This gave her the opportunity to step away from him.

That rare, warm peace ebbed away like a tide rolling back out to sea. Although the sun blazed already hot on her shoulders, she shivered, as if with cold.

"I can see the campus from here, just down the street." Mitch pocketed his keys, his movements confident and relaxed as if he hadn't felt a thing. As if this hadn't affected him this way. "Do you live in the dorms?"

Somehow she managed to make her feet carry her forward as though nothing had happened, as though she were perfectly fine. Her voice came as if from far away. "No, the dorms are too expensive. I have a little apartment three blocks from here."

"Any roommates?"

"Just one."

"An apartment sounds good to me. Right now I have the luxury of living in the barracks."

"The luxury?"

"And so much privacy. Not. I'm happier in a hootch—"

"A hootch?"

"A tent—" he supplied, "in a camp somewhere

overseas with my team. Give me a cot and I'm home. Better yet, I'd rather be sleeping out in the bush."

"Really, on the ground? You like that?"

"Sure. It's like camping, except for the grenades and C4 explosives. I grew up in these mountains."

"Really? The math whiz I remember from high school didn't look like the outdoors type."

"Looks are deceiving, and I was at an awkward age. Okay, a very awkward age. My dad is a forest ranger. We're gonna take one of these weekends I have free—if I get a whole one free—and hike up into the Bridger Mountains. Spend the night. Camp. Cook river trout over a fire."

"Sounds very rugged. I'm more of a stay-away-from-the-mountains kind of girl."

"You just haven't been properly exposed to the wilderness."

"Where there's no hot water, no plumbing and no electric blankets?"

"Those luxuries are highly overrated. Trust me."

"I'm a little afraid to, with an attitude like that."

When she smiled, sweet as candy, his emotions jumbled into a wedge in his throat. The palm of his left hand still glowed from where he'd taken hold of her arm to help her from the Jeep, and the brightness of her touch remained, calming and terrifying all at once.

Heaven was on his side, because Kelly chose that moment to pause in front of a store window. A striped yellow-and-white awning stretched overhead and he studied the way the hem ruffled in the breeze instead of figuring out what was happening to him.

At the back of his mind, he knew. He had a life, he had a calling, and he had eighteen months left on his contract. So how was this going to work?

"The lady who owns this shop is a good friend of the family—well, of Joe's family." Her voice broke on the sound of Joe's name. "She takes antique gems and resets them in the most beautiful jewelry you've ever seen. I don't know if you'd be interested in something like that for your mom, but Holly's work is so beautiful, it's like giving a little piece of love."

Okay, that was the word he was trying to avoid.

"Do you want to go in and look? Or I have other suggestions. We can just go down the block and there's—"

"No, let's start here." It felt like a definite step on an unknown path in the dark, when there was no light to see by. But he wasn't bothered by the dark.

When he opened the door, he wanted to take her by the hand. But he figured she wasn't ready for that. She breezed past him with a rustle of her cotton dress and the tap of her shoes, and he caught again the scent of vanilla and sweetness.

Impossibly, his heart tightened even more.

Chapter Five

Kelly couldn't help leaning closer against the display case to study the brooch Mitch had taken out of its velvet bed. It was an elegant piece of lacy gold with a baguette-cut ruby looking outrageously fragile against Mitch's broad, callused palm.

Stop looking at the man's hand, Kelly told herself. She was supposed to be concentrating on the beautiful pieces of jewelry, right? Not noticing the deep creases in Mitch's palm. Or how capable his fingers looked. The nicks and cuts and scars marred his sun-browned skin. Such powerful hands he had, just like the rest of him.

She *so* remembered the peace his touch had brought her, when he'd helped her from the Jeep.

"What do you think?" His hazel eyes met hers, and in those green and gold depths she saw glimpses of his big heart. He cared about the people in his life—and he cared about her opinion for some reason.

He's just too perfect. If he wasn't, then she wouldn't feel this turmoil seizing her up. Hard lessons learned ought to be enough to make her step away and stay firmly on the path she believed in. The path where God had placed her over and over again.

Mitch waited for her answer, the delicate and expensive brooch resting rock-steady on his palm.

Don't just stand there, Kelly. Say something. Her gaze shot to the other box he'd chosen from among the many in the display cases. Which one did she like better? The dainty necklace shimmered in the sunlight, the delicate swoop of wings and halo around a thumb-nail-sized fresh-water pearl made her heart stop. "It's a pearl. What can I say?"

"You like pearls?"

She supposed he was looking for a woman's opinion on jewelry. "I think your mom might like the ruby better, though."

"You didn't answer my question."

Which question? Her mind wandered. No matter how hard she tried to stop the caring from creeping into her heart, she couldn't. She liked Mitch Dalton. She liked him very much.

As a friend. She couldn't dare think of him as anything else.

"Why pearls?" He studied her, waiting.

Oh, right. Pay attention, Kelly. "Pearls are so

simple and unassuming. Everyone knows that a pearl starts with a tiny grain of sand, but to me, it's like faith. We are like that grain of sand and it's God's grace that can cloak us and make us shine, if we are humble and faithful enough. In the end, it's a thing of true beauty."

"Yes, it certainly is."

He wasn't looking at the pearl. But at her. Somehow his gaze deepened and there he went, somehow feeling too intimate, as if he could see too much. But how could he look past the layers of defense in which she cloaked herself so carefully?

The pieces of her heart stung like salt in a fresh wound, and she felt so vulnerable and wide open. It was Mitch. He made her feel like this. So wouldn't the smartest thing be to head for the door and never look back?

It would be the safest.

"I'll take the ruby," Mitch told Holly, behind the counter. "But could you put the other on hold? I'd like to think about it. Christmas will be here before you know it."

"Sure." Holly gladly set the pearl angel aside and took Mitch's credit card with her over to the cash register.

They were done. Kelly let out a deep breath she wasn't aware she'd been holding. This was how worked up she was. But now Mitch had found his gift, and he'd be heading back to his base.

I'll be back on safe ground.

She probably wouldn't see him again. She didn't want to see him again, right? It wasn't as if she was looking for a man to love—not anymore. Not ever again. It didn't make any sense.

"Mission accomplished." The way he leaned both forearms on the counter, coming in close to her, made her want to hope—past the ache where no hope lived.

How impossible was it to start hoping? And for what? That kind of hope, that kind of dream, was not meant for her. She thought of what had happened with Joe, and it felt as if the shadows within her lengthened. No, this was her path and she would not step one foot off it.

She cleared the thick emotion from her throat. Somehow she managed some resemblance of a normal smile. "Your mom should love the brooch. I bet she'd love anything as long as it was from you."

"Well, she's biased, being my mom. But you, pretty lady, you saved my bacon."

"Me? I just pointed you in the right direction." Why did her heart flutter in her chest? Maybe it was simply the remnants of that old crush. Maybe. She couldn't let it be anything else.

"I did nothing. You would have done fine by yourself, but I'm glad I could help. I wish your mother a very happy birthday. And you a safe journey back to the base tonight."

She took a step in retreat.

"What? You're leaving me? Just like that?"

"You were the one who said mission accomplished."

"Well, maybe there's another mission scheduled after this one."

"Holly gift wraps, so you're good to go." She took another backward step to the door. "Bye, Mitch."

"Wait." As if he was going to let her escape. She was wrong, his mission wasn't close to being completed. Mitch scribbled his signature on the slip the shop owner slid toward him. "Kelly, don't run off on me."

"I've got to study."

"Flimsy excuse." Done, he dropped the pen but Kelly was already heaving open the old-fashioned wood-frame door. The cowbell over the door clanked as she tried to evade him.

Emotion struck him hard in the chest, and he remembered the fear he'd seen in her eyes. "Ma'am, could you wrap this for me? I'll be back."

He hardly registered the owner's agreement; he was already out the door and into the blinding burn of daylight. He turned toward Kelly instinctively, as if he could feel the tug of her spirit against his.

She'd gained some distance on him, he had to give her that. She speed-walked in those purple sandals as efficiently as if they were cross-trainers. The hem of her pretty dress swirled around her slender knees, and her long honey-blond hair swung with her gait, like lustrous liquid gold.

Yeah, she was in definite retreat. What had scared her? He puzzled over that as he bounded after her, cutting around a couple holding hands. She had that strict no-dating outlook on things. Was she bolting because he'd gotten too close? What he needed to know was what had happened with Joe. Otherwise, she was going to run off and he'd never see her again.

Maybe that was as it should be. Maybe it would be best just to let her go. His chest tightened. The tenderness and confused emotions inside him tangled up into an unbreakable knot.

What he did was dangerous. There was no denying it. He'd learned the value of making sure to start each day without regrets. To leave nothing unfinished.

If he let her go, he'd regret it. No doubt about that.

So he continued after her. He could have closed his eyes and found her by heart and by the cadence of her gait. In the reflection of a coffee-shop window he could see her profile, her soft mouth downturned, her chin set with determination. Then her slim shoulders tensed more as if she, too, sensed him behind her. She kept going.

There was a clue, but did he get the hint? No. He kept going. "Kelly? Did I do something wrong?"

"No, you didn't do anything." She spun with a swirl of cotton, stark pain clouding her eyes. "I really do have to study."

"Yeah, but you're running scared, I think. And I

want to know why." He towered over her like a bear.
"Do I scare you?"

She swiped at a shock of blond hair that fell across
her eyes, tucking it delicately behind her ear. He
knew she was biding time, trying to think of the right
answer—one that was still the truth but not the whole
truth, either. She wanted to hold that back, the real
reason she was afraid. Maybe because it was too
personal or too painful.

But if he wanted to have a chance of seeing her
again, then he had to know. He folded his arms over
his chest and waited.

She stared long and hard down at the crack in the
sidewalk between them. "I know you said you
wouldn't mind having a friend, but this doesn't feel
like friendship. I don't know, maybe it's just me. But
there's something—"

He knew exactly what she meant. It should be a
relief that she felt this, too. It wasn't one-sided. But
the tangled mess of emotions in his chest clamped
tight enough to make him wince. "You know what
we can do? Let's find a place to sit down, have lunch
and figure this out."

"Figure what out? I don't want to figure
anything out."

"Running away from this isn't going to make it
go away. Or keep it from happening the next time
we get together."

"The next time?"

"See? That's something else we can talk about. There's a taco place right behind you. How about it?"

"No way am I going to let you turn this into a date, Mr. Dalton." Her words were kind, but strangled. He could see the sadness in her honest blue eyes.

He definitely had to know what had hurt her so much. What had that Joe McKaslin done to her? He thought of all the things that went wrong in the world, in relationships, between two people, that caused that much hurt. Hated to think of her exposed to anything like that. "Why? Why can't you date me?"

"I told you right up front. I have a no-dating policy—"

"And I'm asking why. What happened to you?"

"Life. Just like it happens to everyone else." She lifted her chin, as if determined to hold back her secrets and onto what she felt was private. "Surely you've seen enough of life to know what I'm talking about."

"I have." He pushed aside too many images of the world he'd seen up close. Images so far removed from the safe streets of this little college town and luxury unimagined in some of the places he'd been. But young or old, rich or poor, Christian or not, here or in some desperate country, life happened, and there was no stopping the pain that came right along with the living. "This has to do with Joe."

She took a step back, then another, as if wanting distance. "He's at the Mountain View Cemetery. He's buried there."

"I—I'm sorry. I didn't know."

"Now you do." Kelly's chest clogged tight, as if she were buried under a mountain of snow instead of the pieces of her broken dreams.

She left him standing there, in the middle of the sunswept sidewalk, with life teeming all around him. Students from campus were pacing the sidewalks now that the shops were open. People fresh from church were looking for a place to have lunch and discuss the service. Young mothers pushing strollers and young married couples holding hands, their backpacks heavy on their shoulders as they sought out places to sip coffee and study.

Life swirled all around him, and yet he seemed darker than the shadows.

Kelly felt the same shadows in her soul, and she kept on going, woodenly forcing one foot in front of the other until she'd reached the end of the block. When she turned the corner, he was out of her sight.

But, strangely, not out of her heart. She could feel him there, like the shadows.

And the light.

Okay, that wasn't the answer I expected, Mitch thought, still troubled hours later as he helped clear the dishes from the table. He hadn't forgotten the look in Kelly's eyes—not one of grieving as would be expected—but of hopelessness.

He heard the waltzing rhythm of his mom's gait

in the kitchen behind him. As he gathered up a stack of dinner plates, he tried to put his thoughts aside. His mother could probably sense that he was thinking about a woman, possibly daughter-in-law material. "Don't even think about asking."

"Why? What was I going to ask?" Barbara Dalton paused in the archway and planted a hand on her hip, but the gleam in her eye clearly said, "Fine, I'll just ask later." "Come out onto the deck. Your father is setting up the ice cream maker."

"This'll only take a minute." Like he was going to leave the dishes for his mom to do. "Go help Dad. Go on."

"Who do you think you are, giving orders?" She hefted the stack out of his hands—she was stronger than she looked. "You might be part of an elite force, Sergeant, but in this house you're still my boy and you'll do as I say."

"Yes, ma'am." He liked it when she pulled rank. He loaded up another pile of serving bowls and joined her in the kitchen, where she was stacking the plates in the dishwasher.

"I love my brooch, Mitch." She beamed as she worked. "Wherever did you find it?"

"A little shop near the university."

"You did good." She studied at him as he went in search of the plastic containers she stored leftovers in. "So, is she a nice girl?"

"What makes you think there is one?"

"Mother's intuition."

"Either way, that's filed under the topic of not-your-business."

"Well, I had to try." Mom went back to loading the dishwasher. "I am praying for you to find someone. I would so love a daughter-in-law to spoil."

"I'm still not going to discuss it." He dug a spatula out of a nearby drawer. "Do you remember Joe McKaslin?"

"He went to high school with you, didn't he?" She rinsed flatware beneath the faucet before plunking them into the basket on the bottom rack. "There was something about him in the local paper years ago. He passed away fighting forest fires."

Wow. No wonder he'd felt Kelly's sadness so powerfully.

"So sad, to lose someone that young," his mom went on. "I worry about you every day. You're the reason behind all this gray hair."

"It looks stunning on you, and you shouldn't worry. I can take care of myself." He dropped the container of leftovers in the fridge. "There. Done. What next?"

"Go take those bowls out to your father." She nodded toward the counter. "He should be about ready to dish up."

"Then leave the dishes, Mom. I'll do them later."

"You'll do no such thing. Now go, before I get out my switch."

He laughed at the joke between them, a threat

she'd been using for as long as he could remember and a promise she'd never made good on. He grabbed the bowls and headed to the deck where his dad was fiddling with the lid of the ice cream maker.

Beside him his sister, Suz, a corporate lawyer in Seattle, was out of her area of expertise. "I don't know, Dad. You'll have to ask Mom."

His dad scratched his chin, as if considering the matter. "Maybe Mitch knows."

"He knows nothing," Suz winked at him as he joined them on the deck. "As usual. I'll get Mom."

"Hey now, move aside, Dad." Mitch set the bowls on the patio table and knelt down in front of the ice cream maker. "What's the problem?"

"We'd best wait for your mom. We bust this new-fangled thingy of hers, I'll get in trouble." Dad didn't look too worried as he straightened. "It's good to have you home, son."

"It's good to be here for a change."

Memories surrounded him of all the summers Dad had barbecued on the grill and they'd eaten at the patio table, gazing out at the Bridger Mountains. The pool glittered in the sunshine and beyond the freshly mown lawn evergreens seemed to go on forever. Growing up here had been good; maybe the years to come would be even better.

Why was it, miles away and hours later, he could still feel Kelly in his heart? Because, he suspected, there was a chance that she could be his future.

* * *

Give it up, Kelly. It's no use. She was *not* into studying, no matter how hard she tried to focus. Kelly slammed the book shut and the sound echoed around the dark house. She was babysitting for one of her regulars, Amy—one of Joe's many cousins—and the little ones were snug in bed. When she checked the clock, she realized Amy and her husband would be home in less than an hour.

Why couldn't she concentrate? That was easy, because of Mitch. He was on her mind. Too much and inexplicably. She rubbed the heel of her hand over her hurting heart. Why did Mitch make her feel again in these broken places?

She had no idea. Aimless, she headed into the kitchen. She put a cup of water in the microwave and while it heated, she fished through her backpack until she found the zipper sandwich bag where she kept her teabags. The cinnamon aroma of the tea comforted her, but who was she trying to fool?

Only herself. There could be no comfort for what troubled her tonight. Everything she wanted with all of her soul—it surrounded her in this homey kitchen with bits of love and family everywhere. Crayon drawings and magnetic alphabet letters were tacked on the refrigerator door. Framed snapshots of the babies hung on the walls and were propped on the windowsill over the sink.

The broken pieces of her dreams and of her heart

felt enormous in the comfortable silence of the cozy kitchen. And still, like a survivor beneath an earthquake's rubble, she could feel hope struggling to stay alive in her soul.

Chapter Six

In the middle of reading her assigned sociology chapter, Kelly felt a soft breeze move through her. Awareness flickered to life within her heart, an awareness that was warm and sweet. Highlighter in hand, she looked up over the rail of her top-floor deck, through the rustling, sun-drenched poplar leaves to the street below. A familiar tan Jeep was parked by the curb.

Mitch. Aviator sunglasses hid his eyes and he seemed to gaze along the block. What was he doing here? She hadn't heard from him in a week. She recapped her highlighter and slid out of the plastic deck chair. Remembering how she'd left things between them, part of her was glad to see him, the other part wanted to scrunch down in the chair, hide behind her book and hope he didn't see her.

No such luck. "Hey, Kelly. Are you studying up there?"

"Guilty as charged." She stood, leaving her book open, pages ruffling in the warm breeze.

"It's Saturday evening."

"So? You say that as if it's a bad thing. I like studying." She leaned against the wooden rails. "What are you doing here? And how did you find me?"

"You're listed in the phone book. I know how to read and I am fairly good at finding my way around." He lifted his glasses off his nose enough to meet her gaze. "You went AWOL on me, so I had to hunt you down."

"So, is that a punishable offense?"

"Yep. I've come to impose dinner on you. I hope you like the works, because that's what I got." He withdrew a large pizza box from the back seat. "I'm comin' up."

As if she would want to stop him. "I never say no to a man who comes bearing pizza."

"Lucky me." He piled a cardboard carrier with soda cups and two smaller pizza boxes on top of the one he already carried.

"I like a man who comes prepared."

"Good. I take pizza seriously."

Mitch took one look at her smile, as sunny as the bright summer evening, and the tangle of emotions in his chest yanked so tight he couldn't breathe. She was smiling at him, okay, maybe she was glad to see him…or she really liked pizza, but it was nice to see. As he headed around the small, seventies' apartment building, following the walkways through the mature poplars lining the complex, he spotted Kelly in the open doorway of the top-floor corner unit.

He took in the sweet glint of her dark-blue eyes and her girl-next-door wholesomeness. She looked great with her hair pulled back in a careless ponytail, wearing a light summer T-shirt in the palest shade of blue and comfortable-looking, dark-blue drawstring shorts.

He knew when she'd spotted the flowers because her smile widened. In his enthusiasm, he took the steps two at a time all the way to the top. "I tried calling a couple times, but your line was busy."

"Oh, I was online doing some research at the library. I've got a paper due." She backed into the unit and held the door for him. "I *always* have a paper due, or it seems that way."

She looked nervous. He didn't want that, so he handed her the flowers. "I promise I won't say anything to chase you away this time."

"Deal." She took the bouquet and breathed in the scent of the purple flowers. "I love freesias. How did you know?"

"They just made me think of you. That's a thank you. My mom loved her gift."

"I was glad to help."

He spotted the kitchen straight down the little hallway to the right. Definitely a girl's apartment, he thought as he slid his fragrant load onto the beige-colored counter and nudged a bowl with dried flower stuff aside so the extra-large box would fit. The pepperoni and garlic scent competed with the potpourri. "You haven't eaten yet, have you?"

"No. My shift at the bookstore was over at four-thirty, but I'm waiting for my roommate. We sorta had dinner plans." She joined him in the kitchen and pulled a glass vase from the cabinet beneath the sink. "Do you mind if Lexie joins us?"

"Sure, I'm the one who showed up unannounced."

"Yes, but with pizza and, oh, is that a box of cheesy sticks?" she asked over the rush of the tap water.

"Cheesy sticks and a dessert pizza."

"The blueberry cheesecake swirl one, by chance?"

He nodded confirmation as he removed the drinks from the carrier. "Did I do good?"

"Are you kidding? You did perfect. That's the best pizza in town. Do you mind if we wait? Lexie should be here any minute."

"Sure." He slipped his sunglasses onto the counter. "Pretty nice place you got here."

"Decorated on a budget, but it's home." She unwrapped the flowers and began arranging them in the vase.

He checked out the living area. The furniture was mismatched pieces in different shades of brown and blue, well-worn and comfortable, and aimed at a small wide-screen TV. A sturdy green plastic table sat squarely in the middle of the little deck that looked out over the poplars at the busy street below. A textbook's pages ruffled back and forth in the wind.

"Sit wherever you want," Kelly invited as she arranged the flowers. "How is the mountain-climbing going?"

"I still haven't fallen."

"You must have developed a certain competence at it by now. You said it was an advanced training thing you're doing, right? What's advanced about it?"

"Next week we get to train on glaciers. There's nothing like ice-climbing."

"I haven't ice-climbed in ages." She carried the vase past him to the scarred pine coffee table between a mismatched brown couch and blue striped chair. "Okay, never. It has never occurred to me that people actually climb across mountain glaciers."

"Well, they do if they want to get to the other side."

"Tell me that's not your idea of a joke."

"My sense of humor. It's why no woman will have me."

Oh, I doubt that, Kelly thought as she studied him. She imagined plenty of nice women would definitely consider him a fine catch.

The door opened, and Lexie's voice filled the little foyer. "Kelly? I couldn't believe it! I got the last copy on the shelf—"

Kelly watched her roommate skid to a stop midsentence, stunned by the sight of the guy standing in their living room. Before Lexie could jump to the wrong conclusion, Kelly made it clear. "Mitch and I went to the same high school. He's an old acquaintance, because we were never really friends. I was too shy."

"So was I," Mitch added, slipping his hands into his back pockets, which only emphasized the corded muscles in his arms. "It's good to meet you."

"You, too." Lexie swiped a chunk of wayward black hair behind her ear and looked utterly shocked. "I, uh, am just on my way back out. You two have a nice date—"

"Not a date," Kelly emphasized. "Mitch and I were waiting for you. He brought cheesy sticks. C'mon, let's grab some plates."

His ego was *not* getting a boost. Good thing he was tough, Mitch thought. There was nothing a guy liked better than being a friend, when that wasn't what he had in mind at all.

But it really was, he realized. The least he wanted with Kelly was friendship, and that was a good place to start. He noticed the rental DVD case the roommate was holding. "Is it movie night?"

"You can stay and watch it with us." Kelly offered, handing him a plate over the counter. "Lexie, did you say that you got the last copy?"

"Yeah, of the new romantic comedy that just came out for rent." Lexie still looked uncertain, even as she dumped her backpack and the video case on the edge of the couch. "I bet you're not into romantic comedies, Mitch."

"Not my thing, but I'm up for it."

He really was a nice guy. Kelly knew he probably wasn't jumping for joy to spend his Saturday evening watching a girl movie, but he was here as a friend. He'd come all this way—maybe he really was lonely, just as he'd said last week, when he'd brought burgers for her dinner break.

She was glad he'd come. "This is so much better than what we had planned. Barbecued hot dogs on our hibachi. Thanks, Mitch, for bringing the pizza."

"And the cheesy sticks." Lexie chimed in as she started loading up her plate.

"Any time, ladies."

Yeah, Kelly couldn't help thinking, he was *definitely* one of the good guys.

Nightfall darkened the dome of the sky as Kelly opened the door. "You were a good sport about the movie."

"It had some funny parts. It was a nice, wholesome movie. It was good for me."

"I doubt that, but thanks for coming. Maybe you'll want to stop by again."

"If that's an invitation, I'll take you up on it. Say, next Saturday night. I'll bring pizza again, if you want."

"My treat since you brought this time. We're friends, remember?"

"All right, then." Somehow, he would survive this friendship thing. He hesitated on the top step. "Same time same place next week?"

"I'd really like that." She trailed him out onto the covered landing. "It's pretty late. You have a long drive back."

"Don't worry about me. I've only been up and going full-bore since oh-five-hundred."

"Your hours seem as long as mine. Except ice-climbing is sadly lacking from my daily workout regime."

"You don't know what you're missing."

"Seeing as I'm more of an indoor girl, I'm more than happy to pass on the glacier-climbing. You really like it?"

"I do." That was an understatement. He started down the steps, slowly, going backward so he could watch Kelly standing in the shower of light from inside the door. "Monday, when you notice the whitecaps on the highest mountains, think of me."

"I'll send a whole bunch of no-slipping prayers your way."

"I'd appreciate it." Mitch stopped at the landing, gazing up the length of steps between them. It was late, he needed to head back but the last thing he wanted to do was to go. "How's the math class?"

"Good, but then I haven't looked at that homework all day. When I crack that book tomorrow, I'll be singing a different tune."

"You having trouble with the class?"

"It's math. Math equals trouble. Wait, you love the subject, so you don't understand delaying torture whenever possible."

"You just don't have the right attitude when it comes to math. You wouldn't happen to have a pen handy?"

"You're not going to look at my homework, are you?" Her brows knitted and made an adorable crinkle between her eyes. "It's late. It's Saturday night. I have a strict no-math policy on Saturday nights."

"You have a lot of strict policies. First no dating, and now no math on certain nights. I'll be back in town tomorrow. Mom's dragging me to church with her and Dad so she can show her friends I really do exist and I'm not a figment of her imagination."

"You don't make it home much, I take it?"

"I've made it home for one Christmas, and about ten days total, and that's after boot camp. I spend ninety-nine percent of my life on a mission or waiting for one. Hey, how about I give you my cell number and my e-mail address? You can call if you want me to stop by. Or just e-mail a question."

"You've got to be kidding. You're busy enough."

"Sure, but I always have time for my friends. And for the thrill of math."

"All right, hot shot, but don't say I didn't warn ya."

"Bring it on. I'm used to a certain amount of hardship."

Kelly darted inside to grab the little spiral notepad by the phone. As she scavenged around the kitchen for a pen, delicate freesias scented the air with incredible sweetness.

"Use mine," Lexie offered, hopping up from the couch to hand over a purple glitter-gel pen. "He's awesome. You should date him."

Kelly shook her head. "Too complicated. He's leaving soon. He's stationed in California. Plus, I'm done with romance."

"Bummer." Lexie returned to the couch where the TV droned the latest local news.

Bummer was an understatement, but that was life.

Kelly stepped out onto the front porch and her gaze found Mitch by feel rather than by sight. He'd retreated to the darker corner of the landing, but he radiated such a strong essence of might and honor that she saw him clearly, even when the twilight shadows hid his features.

She came closer and could just make him out leaning against the railing, his arms crossed over his chest. The embers within her heart breathed to life. Just a flicker, but it was bright and joyful.

This is happiness, she told herself. Mitch was a good friend, the pizza-bringing, kindly, offering-to-help-her-with-her-homework type of friend. Why shouldn't she feel gladdened by that?

Mitch met her halfway, reaching out for the pad and pen. "If I hear you had trouble and you didn't ask me for help, I'm gonna be pretty mad at you."

She wasn't fooled; she spotted the good-natured crook of his grin, even in the shadows. "It's my strict policy never to get someone as big and strong as you mad at me."

"Good policy." His grin widened as he wrote and handed her back the book and pen. "I'll provide the movie next time. Deal?"

"Something PG."

"There's a challenging mission, but lucky for you, I always prevail. Good night, Kelly."

"Night. Drive safe."

He raised one hand in answer, moving down the stairs silently. Not even the bottom step squeaked as he disappeared from her sight, taking the brightness of his presence with him.

In his Jeep, heading north over the moon-drenched Montana landscape, Mitch thought over the evening. Not bad. It had gone much better than he had the right to hope for. Kelly had relaxed around him, especially with her roommate there.

Over pizza consumed at the balcony table, with the rustling trees, the wind and sun, he'd asked questions about college life. About Kelly's life. He learned that she worked full-time at the bookstore and supplemented that with babysitting jobs. That she was a straight-A student. She was starting to do extra study for the exams to get into graduate school. And that she daintily picked green peppers off her pizza.

She amazed him. Life had brought her a lot of twists and turns. The image of her standing on the top step, the light from the apartment behind her, the moon's glow falling over her in the dark night, remained. She was pretty determined that all the two of them had in store was friendship.

He considered her side of things. It sounded as if she'd been alone for most of her formative years. And just when she thought she'd found a place to belong and someone to love, it had been ripped from her.

Pretty devastating. No wonder Kelly had given up on dating. On trying to find love again. No wonder the friendship-only thing was so important. He could understand that. He knew what deep losses could do to a person. Closing your heart off kept you from getting too close and feeling too much. It was easier.

But it was no way to live.

Plus the tangled-up emotion in his chest had little to do with friendship feelings. Tonight he'd really felt at home on the couch beside her, with his feet up on the coffee table. He'd enjoyed the simplicity of sitting at her side, and it had felt right. He'd like to spend a lot more evenings just like that. But not as just her friend.

As the highway unrolled before the reach of the Jeep's headlight, Mitch thought how life resembled his limited view. You just couldn't see what was up ahead. Life came with risks and love did, too. You had to give with your whole heart, but you were really just driving in the dark. The turns and obstacles ahead were a mystery, veiled in the night, and you just couldn't know how things would work out.

All you could do was to walk in faith and not hold back.

Chapter Seven

Doom.

Kelly looked up from her textbook and rubbed her tired eyes. The living room came slowly into focus. Two hours of struggling with the mysteries of algebra, mysteries which she had purposefully forgotten over the years, and the truth, as solid as ever, stared her right in the face. The final regular test of the summer quarter was getting closer and she wasn't going to pull an A. She'd be lucky to get a C the way she was going, and that would pull down her entire average.

Definitely doom.

Mitch's kindly spoken words echoed through her mind and right into her heart. *If I hear you had trouble and you didn't ask me for help, I'm gonna be pretty mad at you.*

Since it was a bright late-Monday afternoon, and

Mitch was probably out pick-axing his way up a glacier, she opted for an e-mail instead of calling.

It took just a second to type up an outgoing message to the address he'd given her, as it was only one word: Help! She signed off, including her cell number since she was scheduled to babysit tonight.

The twists God put in a man's path were an amazing thing, Mitch thought as he dialed Kelly's cell number. It had to be no coincidence that he loved math—always had—and that he was in the position to offer her the one thing she'd accept from him—help for her upcoming test. Proof that he was on the right path.

After the third ring, her voice filled the line, dulcet and low as a whisper. "Mitch?"

"Hey, I got your SOS. I would have called you sooner, but we just got in."

"You've been out all day? It's nine o'clock."

"I don't work banker's hours. I'm just lucky I don't have to sleep on the ground tonight. Mountainsides are generally rocky. Not so comfortable. Where are you?"

"Babysitting. Actually, the kids are asleep and so I'm studying, but it's a disaster."

"You've got the right man." He intended to show her that. "What's the problem?"

"If only it were that uncomplicated. I have a test in a week, the last one before finals and it's a big part of my grade. I'm not getting what to do with quadratic equations. It's eluding me."

"Sounds like you're in need of a tutor."

"I am. What are your rates?"

"Barbecue a couple of hot dogs on your hibachi and we'll call it even."

"That's what I had planned for Saturday's dinner."

"I'll come early, we'll get your math crisis figured out before dinner. Sound like a deal?"

"A very good one. How was the ice-climbing?"

"Cold." His chuckle was cut short. There was some noise going on in the background. "Oh, I've gotta go. We've got a surprise field exercise."

"It's almost ten at night."

"Welcome to my world. I'll be at your place, uh, around four-thirty. See ya." The line disconnected.

Kelly sat alone in Amy's living room and stared at the phone, his voice, his words echoing in her head. *Why does he affect me so strongly, Lord?*

No answer came. The brightness Mitch brought to her spirit faded in slow increments with each breath.

And only shadows remained.

Mitch. She couldn't help thinking of him throughout the week. Things would happen that brought him to the forefront of her mind. Driving to work and seeing the highest snowcapped peaks of the Rockies rimming the northwestern horizon, and those glaciers glinting in the hot late-August sun made her wonder if Mitch was out on a snowy peak like those, climbing to his heart's content.

Every time she cracked open her math book or sat in the auditorium class: while she wasn't looking forward to facing a tutoring session, she was glad about her tutor.

Who would have guessed all those years ago that the shy, out-of-place foster girl and the smart, awkward math geek from a middle-class life would wind up being friends? Or that he would be helping her once again?

God worked in funny ways. But she wasn't going to question it. She knew the Lord's hand had been gently guiding them together. Why else would her heart come back to life a little? Why else was she starting to feel a brightness inside her, after Joe's loss had taken it all?

During her shift at the bookstore today, both Katherine and Spence had asked her how things were going with the soldier. Really, they had it all wrong, but when each had asked about him, she started thinking about him all over again. How funny he could be, and how his chuckle rolled like warm joy, low and deep, just the way a friend's laugh should be.

The best part was that she was going to see him in a few minutes. She was running a little early, so she'd have time to get some iced tea made before he came. In a hurry, she whipped into one of the several parking spots in front of her staircase.

Her soul stirred. Strange. She squinted through the windshield to the top landing above. And there, through the shield of poplars swaying in the wind was a silhouette, tall and dependable and waiting for her. Her shining knight—er, tutor.

Like the sunshine streaming through the flickering leaves, her day brightened. She hopped out of the car, bringing her backpack and keys with her. "Hey, stranger. You're early."

"Better than being late." He braced his hands on the rail and leaned, gazing down at her. His smile was wide and friendly, and she knew his eyes were too, behind those aviator sunglasses he wore. He was dressed in jeans again, and a navy-blue T-shirt. "I've only been waiting a few minutes. Are you ready to be put through your paces?"

"Ugh. I knew I was going to regret this. I've been putting off even dealing with anything mathematical all week. It's going to be torture, isn't it?"

"Well, I am a marine. We show no mercy."

"Just my luck." She climbed upward, feeling as light as air. "Lexie wanted me to ask. What movie did you bring?"

"No way. Homework first. Then we'll talk movies."

"Whew, you are demanding." She was close enough to see that there was a military logo on the chest of his T-shirt, and the deep-navy color made his eyes a dark, fathomless green.

Not that she was noticing. "Hey, when you had to get off the phone when we were talking last week— did everything turn out okay?"

"Our CO—commanding officer—thought it would be funny to order us out on a midnight climb."

"In the dark?"

"Well, when you're doing what I do, they don't want you seen. It kind of interferes with the stealthy part of the job. We do a lot of training stuff at night because we do a lot of our missions through the night."

"Missions. That's like what, hanging off cliffs and crossing glaciers? Do you know what?" She unlocked her front door. "I'm starting to suspect that you aren't a normal soldier."

"I told you. I'm like a scout. I do reconnaissance."

"*Like* a scout." Yeah, that was so revealing—not. She opened the door and led the way to the kitchen. "Okay, you keep saying that. You're *like* a scout, but what do you do, exactly? You climb mountains, scuba dive, do amphibious stuff. You're not like Special Forces, are you?"

She feared she knew the answer already.

He shrugged one muscled shoulder, as if it were no big deal. "I'm a Force Recon marine."

Oh, the humble thing was so appealing. Kelly tried to keep her heart still as she took out two cans of soda from the fridge and handed him one. "I don't know what that is. Explain, please."

"Thanks." He popped the top of the can. "We're the elite of the elite. Force Recon is basically the on-the-ground eyes. We patrol enemy territory and act as scouts so our guys know what they're getting into."

"Enemy territory? Like you scout out enemy soldiers?" She took a sip of the icy bubbling cola. It kept her from saying that he looked pretty sane for a crazy person. She tried to imagine how dangerous that had to be. "You need to ice-climb *just* to find out the other side's position? No, you do more than scout, don't you?"

"Yeah. We're pretty big and bad." He shrugged that shoulder again. Apparently that was all he was saying. "Ready to get to it?"

"Math? Sure." Her backpack was still hanging from her shoulder. "We can stay in here, where the air conditioning is, I can turn it up. Sorry." She headed toward the thermostat and adjusted the dial. "Or we can sit outside. Oh, and there's a park a few blocks down."

"The deck is good. I don't want to get too far away from the food."

"I get the hint. Hungry?"

"I could be."

"That's just a hungry man's way of being polite." She grabbed a bag of chips and handed it to him. "Do you like French onion or ranch?"

"Yes."

"I should've known." She grabbed both dip tubs from the fridge and followed him out onto the deck. "Appetizers."

"There's no better." He opened the bag. "Are you ready?"

She tugged her math book out of her pack. It had been a long time since she'd been this happy at heart, especially when it came to algebra.

Mitch's friendship was turning out to be a true blessing in her life.

As Mitch knelt on the deck boards to turn the franks grilling on the hibachi, he could see Kelly's reflection in the large window. She was leaning forward over her plate to scoop her chip through the dip. Her face was turned in profile as she talked with her roommate.

When it came to Kelly, there couldn't be a prettier woman on earth. Not in his opinion. Her golden hair was down today, rippling in the warm breeze and caressing the creamy curves of her face. She wore a sleeveless blouse the exact blue of her eyes, and a black pair of walking shorts and matching shoes. She looked casual and wholesome and womanly all at once.

It really wasn't fair that he was at such a disadvantage.

I hope You know where You're leading me, Lord, because I'm in over my head. He cared for her more than he felt safe admitting, even to himself. He tonged the hot dogs from the grill and onto a plate. "Seconds?"

"It's nice having such first-rate service, thanks."

Kelly smiled up at him as she swiped mustard on a bun. "You have great grill skills."

"I've put in a lot of hard practice at the barbecue."

He slid a beef frank onto Lexie's plate before he added the last two to his. Across the table, Kelly was pushing the relish and mustard in his direction. Her fingers were long, slender and delicate, like the rest of her. Her short nails were painted a light pink.

Lexie shoved the tub of deli potato salad closer. "So, Mitch, tell us exactly why you aren't married."

"Because I spend pretty much most of my time on a mission or on standby prepared to head out. It doesn't leave a lot of time for finding a nice lady to marry." He cast a glance sideways at Kelly. "This free time I have—real weekends—is a luxury."

Lexie persisted. "Yeah, but you'd like to get married one day, right?"

"Sure. I just haven't slowed down enough to let a woman catch me and shackle me into matrimony. Yet."

"Shackle?" Kelly questioned with the cute little crinkle at the bridge of her nose.

"That's a totally typical man's answer." Lexie didn't seem too happy with him.

He shrugged, running a line of mustard along both hot dogs. "Apparently a guy should never joke about the seriousness of marriage in front of women."

"Ya think?" Lexie frowned at him, but her eyes said something different. Like she was on to him.

"Let me try again." He set down the mustard bottle so he could concentrate. He didn't want to get it wrong this time. "I'd like to get married one day. I'm taking my time because I want to find the real thing."

"Real love." Lexie nodded her tentative approval. "Don't we all want to find that?"

I think I already have, he thought. All he had to do was to look at Kelly and his heart did funny things, leaving him feeling exposed and vulnerable.

That just couldn't be good. "Is this how you two spend every Saturday evening?"

"Just about," Kelly answered between dainty bites. "Unless I have a babysitting job."

"But mostly it's a budget meal and a rented movie," Lexie concluded.

"The reality of putting yourself through college." Kelly didn't seem to mind. "On the Saturdays after payday, we splurge and order a pizza."

"You live large. I'm guilty of the same kind of lifestyle." Mitch stole more chips from the bag in the center of the table.

"We're flush. Lexie, remember last January? We were both flat-broke from paying tuition, I'd lost my retail job due to layoffs after Christmas, and we couldn't scrape enough money together between the two of us for rent."

"My dad's check was lost in the mail, it really was, and he was out of the country," Lexie explained, "so we were, like, digging out the pennies from the bottoms of our book bags and purses."

"And on the floor of the car," Kelly added. "Sure, it's funny now, but let's just say there was a big sale on cases of those cups of instant noodles at the discount grocery. It's practically all we ate for three weeks."

"So," Mitch guessed, "you're telling me not to take you out for noodles?"

"Exactly." She laughed. "I'm definitely noodled out."

Her laughter lightened his world. His voice didn't sound like his own as he made a suggestion. "I saw that a couple of good movies were playing down at the old theater. I thought I'd treat you girls to popcorn and a movie. Interested?"

Kelly's gaze met his, and, like a spark to kindling, he felt the impact.

"That would be very nice," she said and her smile moved like sunlight through him.

He had to admit that he cared for her. It wasn't a conscious decision and there wasn't much he could do about it.

With the warm still air and star-studded ebony sky, the August evening felt like a dream. Or, Kelly conceded, maybe it was the man she was walking with. Something about being with Mitch made her world better.

"Are you sure we shouldn't have waited for your roommate?" Mitch asked. "It's dark and she shouldn't be walking alone."

"I have a feeling that guy she ran into at the concession stand has been wanting to date her for a long time. I bet he'll give her a ride home." It was nice of him to be concerned, though, Kelly thought. See? It just went to show what a thoughtful guy he was. "What you did this evening, helping me figure out my math, is a big deal to me. You may have saved my grade point average."

"Well, not yet. The test is tomorrow."

"But now I've nailed every practice test question the prof handed out. I couldn't do one of them before you came today."

"Ah, you could too. You were just getting psyched out about it. I didn't do much."

"It's a lot to me."

"I'm glad I could help." Mitch rewarded her with his charming, lopsided grin, the one that made her spirit light up.

She couldn't remember a nicer thing, simply walking like this at his side. Maybe it's the gorgeous night, she reasoned, the hush of their footsteps on the sidewalk in perfect synchronicity and the quarter-moon peering over the city so that they walked in its platinum glow.

Or, maybe it was the man—wait, correct that—*friend* at her side.

Companionable silence mantled them as they walked down quiet streets. The bright lights of some of the college dorm windows were visible through the trees lining the sidewalk, and, as they turned the corner and crossed the road, the curtained windows of homes stretched for blocks.

Mitch broke the stillness. "I've got only two more weekends left before they drag me back to my base."

"Two more?" She'd known that, of course, but to hear the words out loud hit like a punch.

"Dad and I are going up into the national park next Friday to spend the night. I want to do that before I head out. With this thing going on in the Middle East, I'm gonna be hard-core, and I don't know…I might not make it back until I'm discharged eighteen months from now."

She'd known that, so why did it feel as if she were choking on disappointment?

"It'll mean a lot to Dad, and to me, too. But I've got Sunday afternoon free. You're gonna need to take a study break, right?"

She cleared the emotion from her throat, but her voice sounded thick anyway. "Are you kidding? Finals start in a week. I'll be half-comatose. I'll need a serious study break."

"Something fun."

"What does a guy who hangs off of mountains for a living do for *fun?*"

"There's hang gliding."

"Are you serious? I can't do heights."

"How about BASE jumping?"

"*What?* I'd have to be insane, and I'm not there yet."

"Ice-climbing is out?"

"Don't go there, I'm warning you." Although she sounded almost stern, the hint of a dimple at the corners of her mouth showed, even when she was doing her best to keep from grinning.

"All right. How about this: if you get an A on your test, I pick. You get a B or less, then you can pick what we do."

"I'm only agreeing to this because I don't think there's any way that I'll actually pull an A. The only problem is that I have a babysitting gig at six."

Mitch realized they'd stopped in the shadow of her building. There was his Jeep parked a few car lengths up the curb. Disappointment set in. He didn't like the idea of having to leave her. "We'll have you to your babysitting thing on time."

"How about I'll meet you at the city park around noon, and I'll bring my graded test. We'll take it from there."

"The west entrance." He jammed his hand into his jeans pocket and pulled out his keys. Sorting through the ring gave him something to focus on when he really wanted to do nothing more than brush his lips with hers, gently kiss her soft, rosebud mouth so she would know how he felt.

But she wasn't ready for that. She wasn't ready for more.

Yet.

He didn't blame her. He could relate. This was a scary, unknown path. Especially to a marine who was trained to be swift, silent and deadly, but when it came to *this*—matters of the heart—he wasn't so capable.

He walked backward so he could keep her in his sight. "Thanks for a good evening."

"I should be thanking you. Safe journeys, Mitch."

"Night." He could walk away, but he couldn't stop his tenderness for her that burned like a rocket's glare in the dead of night.

He didn't know where this was leading. He only knew that God was leading him.

He would trust in that.

Chapter Eight

"Are you having fun yet?"

Fun? Kelly studied Mitch over the rim of the giant inner tube she held on to for dear life, although the cool lapping eddy of the river's edge only came to her knees. Fun? That settled it, he was definitely certifiable.

The trouble was, he looked anything but. In running shorts and a military-green tank top, he radiated complete ease and self-assurance as he waded ahead of her into the deeper pull of the current.

I'd have to be crazy to follow him.

She took another step along the rocky river bottom—putting her sanity in serious question.

She squinted through the blinding sunlight bouncing off the wide river's surface at the intrepid man who obviously had no common sense. "This *can't* be your idea of fun."

"You'd better believe it." He stopped waist-deep

in the mountain-fed river and took hold of her inner tube. "That's some death grip you got there. Relax. I won't let anything happen to you."

"Promises, promises." She cast her gaze down river, contemplating all the ways she could drown.

"Don't tell me you're afraid of water, too."

"Okay, I won't tell you." She bit her bottom lip to keep in the squeak of fear that erupted the moment he gave an effortless jerk on her inner tube and kept pulling. Her feet lifted off the rocky riverbed as he drew her through the eddies and directly into the teeth of the current. The force of it seemed to bite like a dog, held on and tried to drag her away. Not the best sensation.

Help? She couldn't seem to make that word come out of her terror-struck mouth. She wasn't aware how it happened, but he was at her side and his steely arm drew her toward him.

Their inner tubes bumped together and she jostled to a stop against him. There she was, in the shelter of his arms, up to her chin in water, protected from the river's tenacious current and shaded from the blinding sun. Safe at his side, her fear trickled away into nothing at all.

Her feet found a firm purchase on the rocks below and a different fear coursed through her as he casually drew her closer still. Somehow she found enough air to breathe in order to speak. "I thought we were going wading or something."

"That'll teach you to jump to conclusions."

"No, it was more like wishful thinking. Clinging to false hopes."

"You do know how to swim, right?" Mitch could feel the way she trembled. Tenderness flowed through him with a force that was greater than the river, greater than anything he'd ever known before.

The emotion sharpened until it ached in his throat. She was so little and fragile and dainty in his arms, and that well of tenderness just kept on brimming. He wished he could hold her close and protect her. Forever.

The question was, would she let him?

He tugged her a little closer, but she seemed to resist. That was his answer, apparently. Okay, he'd work with that.

"I know enough to dog paddle basically." There was that cute furrow again between her eyes. The one he wanted to kiss until her worry went away. He doubted that would make her calmer right now. In time, he thought, although it was tough not being able to take this up a level.

Was it his imagination, or did she cling to him more tightly? His care for her was like nothing he'd ever known before. He longed to be with her in the way mountaintops needed snow, rivers needed the sea. The way night needed the dawn. To feel whole. With a perfect purpose.

Ever since he'd left for boot camp, he'd found a great purpose to his life. One he felt qualified and called to do. But right now, being with Kelly, his whole heart crumpled and fell, changing him forever.

"Don't worry. I'll be right with you," he promised. "I'm qualified in water stuff."

"Water stuff? That makes me feel so much better. *Not.*"

"It should. I'm trained in all sorts of amphibious things. You're in good hands. Ready?"

No, she was *so* not ready. Kelly gave a squeak of fear as she was whisked up onto the seemingly enormous inner tube, which he held safely for her. As aggressively as the current tried, it could not tear her away from Mitch's grip.

This was a very bad idea. Panic roared through her with a quaking iciness, stealing the hot burn from the sun on her face and arms, and drowning out the rush of the river. It wasn't the river that was scaring her now. *That* fear, as great as it was, was nothing compared to the panic threatening to take her over. It was Mitch. Her feelings for him were so strong.

He made it all worse with the gentle brush of heat as he leaned to whisper in her ear. "No worries. I'll keep you safe. Count on me."

It would be so totally tempting to care for him in a way that went beyond friendship, Kelly thought as she clutched the side of the rubber inner tube. Mitch looked like everything trustworthy in the world—he was strong of character and spirit. As a friend, he made her laugh, but he did more than that. He lit up her world.

What could she do about that? She'd stop feeling this way, that's what. She'd hold on tight to her common sense, that's what. At least her panic was in perspective. She studied the roll and hiss of the wide, fast-moving river. Whatever danger it held for her was nothing like the peril of letting herself care too much for this man.

"Just hold on, whatever happens," he advised.

As if any force on earth could possibly be stronger than her grip! If she could lower the panic level enough to speak, she'd tell him that.

"And don't forget to enjoy the ride." He looked way too confident, as if there wasn't a bit of danger.

Help, he was nuts. "I'm not sure about this, Mitch," she choked out. Translation: Let me off.

"That's only because you've never ridden rapids before."

"There's a reason for that."

"Sure, but you'll have the best time, and once you do, you'll want to do it over and over again."

"I seriously doubt I'll suddenly turn that loony."

She wanted to gaze at the shore with longing—if only she could see it. But her stubborn eyes wouldn't look past Mitch. She couldn't see anything but the solid granite lines of his face, the trustworthy honor that burned steadily in his hazel eyes and the unyielding strength as he held her safely against the river's might. His chuckle shot through her like winter thunder.

Every instinct within her shrieked at her to run

to higher ground, quick, before he let go, before she was dashed on the rapids that lay ahead like a hungry predator.

But it was too late. Before she could protest, he was pushing her and her inner tube more deeply into the river, toward the hungry, gurgling, dangerous current. The rocky beach floated farther away, and safety with it. The undercurrent grew ferocious, sucking at her feet, which were dangling off the end of the tube. The river's gurgle became a menacing low-throated growl.

Okay, time to get off now.

"M-Mitch?" She couldn't believe it. He'd released his hold on her inner tube. He was letting her go.

While the current sped her away from him, she watched him helplessly. Water sluiced off his sun-browned skin as he hopped onto his tube. He stretched out on the inflated tube with easy confidence, as if nothing rattled him, nothing troubled him, as if he could do anything.

Her feelings for him were absolutely without a doubt way too strong. She clutched the slippery sides of the tube, fighting down panic on many levels, and floated into the jet stream of the current. She sped along so fast that the world whirred by in a blur of green cottonwoods and amber wild grasses dry from the midsummer sun, the green grass of the city park and the clean pure blue of the river.

Her feelings were speeding along too, out of control, just like this inner tube she couldn't stop if she tried—no brakes. The rapids were imminent, she could clearly see the upcoming white crests of water splashing over and around black protrusions of big river rocks. She was going to hit them.

Oh, Lord, don't let me hit them.

God didn't seem to answer—how could He hear her over the roar of the river? And suddenly there was a bump against the back of her inner tube. Mitch had caught up with her. He'd come to save her.

"Fun, right?" His wide, happy smile was a grin of a man who lacked all common sense. "You ain't seen nothing yet. Hold on!"

Hold on? To what? He was nuts. Absolutely nuts.

Her fingers squeaked along the rubber tubing as she tried to get a better grip. The river bucked up like a wild bronco and then bowed back down and up again, whirling her backwards and tossing her up into the air like the worst carnival ride. Suddenly she was spinning toward a fast-approaching hunk of granite that looked very capable of breaking her bones if she rammed into it.

But at the last minute, the white-frothing water steered her to the side of the boulder and with a swoosh rolled her around another. Somewhere behind her Mitch was whooping like a kid on a fair ride, but she couldn't see anything except the swirling water turning to bubbling foam. The rapids tossed her up and down without end, as if trying to shake her bones from her body.

With a last surge of effort, the river reared a final time, tossing her upward with such force that she soared into the hot summer air. Wow, it was like flying. The black ring of rubber shot from beneath her and out of sight and she was falling, gravity-bound, watching the swirling water rising up to meet her in a cool splash of wetness. It was like landing in happiness, then she was sinking deep.

A steely hand caught her forearm and stopped her descent. Mitch's hand, Mitch's touch, his protection as she whooshed to the surface, her pulse pounding with joy. Water sluiced down her face and she drew in a mouthful of air, laughing, as Mitch held her steady, treading water.

"You're right. That was fun." She swiped a wet hank of hair out of her eyes to see him more clearly.

Maybe for the first time. His short dark hair was plastered to his head and seemed to accent the strong high blades of his cheekbones, his straight nose and granite jaw.

But as he gathered her in his arms and helped her ashore, where her inner tube drifted, trapped against the bank, it was his touch that affected her. The shadows within her faded, and there was only light.

"How about another run?" Mitch asked, humor glinting in his hazel eyes because he already knew the answer.

Okay, so he'd been right. "I'll beat you there." She hooked her inner tube and started running along the grassy shore.

Hours later, Mitch took another bite of his hand-dipped ice-cream cone. Walking through the grassy public park with Kelly was pretty nice. "This has to be one of the best things on earth."

"This? An ice-cream cone?" The lowering slant of the sunlight brushed her with bronze. She tipped her head back, scattering the long, damp locks of golden hair. "It *is* good, but it's just an ice-cream cone."

"Are you kidding? This chocolate crust is real dark chocolate. The cone is bakery quality, it doesn't come out of a box. You can't get this just anywhere."

"It's good, sure." She ate her cone by peeling off the thick chocolate layer first, eating it piece by piece. "But there are probably thousands of places that sell something like this or better."

"See, you take it for granted." He resisted the urge to touch the wayward locks whipping in the wind across her face, to feel the silken strands against his palm. "That's because you can pick up an ice-cream cone all the time. When I'm deployed, I don't get things like this."

"And that makes it one of the best things on earth?" Kelly picked another curve of chocolate off the top of her cone. She was smirking, as if he greatly amused her.

"It's probably not one of the *very* best things, but it goes on my list anyway."

"What list?"

"The one I keep in my head. For nights when I'm with my team and we're hunkered down on some remote mountain in a blizzard, wet to the skin and half-frozen. There's no fire because we don't want the smoke and the flames. No tent, no dry clothes, nothing but a meal in a can. That's when I haul out my list and try to remember all the good things, so it doesn't seem as bad."

"Remembering ice cream is going to make you feel better in a blizzard?"

"Okay, right. I'll save that for the desert list. When it's 123 degrees in the shade, except there is no shade, then I'll remember this afternoon. How the river was cooling—not too cold, just right. The way you laughed when I pulled you up after the rapids. How this feels right now, eating ice cream and walking with you."

"It's the ice cream you'll remember. Not me." She blushed prettily.

Yep, he was hooked. Something more powerful than tenderness filled him up until it felt impossible to breathe. "Oh, I think there's a fair-to-middling chance I'll remember you."

Like he could ever forget.

He caught a dripping edge of his ice cream, but the rich crunchy outside and the melting chocolate center wasn't what filled his senses. "You could write to me, when I'm away. Right?"

"Write to you? Well, I suppose I *could* be persuaded."

"Okay, what'll it take? How about a burger with the works at that stand over there?"

"We just ate ice cream."

"But it's nearly five o'clock. I believe in eating dessert first."

"I believe in eating dessert any time you can." Kelly managed to keep her tone light, although her heart wasn't—not at all. She didn't want to think of him leaving.

"I'm going to miss—" She couldn't quite say the words.

"Yeah, me too." Without words, he understood.

Without words, they walked together, side by side. When he took her hand in his, it was all she could do to hold closed the locks on her already adoring heart.

Could it be true? Was the baby finally asleep?

With the infant snuggled in her arms, Kelly eased the rocking chair to a stop and studied Shannon's sweet cherub's face. Her eyes were closed, her rosebud mouth relaxed, lost in dreams. Her warm weight felt utterly limp as she breathed in a slow, sweet rhythm.

It was amazing someone so small could cry so

loud and long, but how could Kelly mind? Holding the little one and rocking her until she calmed was a precious thing. After all, teething, even with all the ways to soothe tender gums, was painful business.

As she carefully rose from the comfy chair, she watched to make sure that the baby didn't stir. With love, she eased Shannon into her snug crib, adorned with the cutest patterned sheets, and dodged the rainbow-colored mobile dangling overhead.

It would be so easy to start dreaming, Kelly thought, standing over the crib, not quite able to take a step away. Already her heart was forming a wish she could not give life to. And it was Mitch's fault for being so wonderful, so everything a girl like her could ever want.

At least she had good control over her heart. The last time she'd made fairy-tale wishes for true love Joe had been taken from her. She'd learned her lesson the hard way too many times. Fairy tales weren't real.

Taking care not to make a sound, she stepped back until she reached the doorway. So far so good. Since the baby didn't stir, Kelly continued on, padding quietly down the hall, past the older child's bedroom door, closed tight while he slept.

She made her way to the kitchen, and she couldn't help the happiness rising up inside her. What a wonderful day she'd had. Not only had she aced her test, thanks to a few extremely important pointers from Mitch last week, but she'd had the best time with him.

Her spirit still felt uplifted as she ran hot soapy water in the sink and started washing up the supper dishes. The faint aroma of frozen pepperoni pizza lingered in the air as she scrubbed the stubborn baked-on cheese off the cookie sheet.

She was rinsing the soap off when a faint electronic tune sounded in the far corner of the room, from her half-unzipped backpack slung over one of the kitchen chairs. Who would be calling her this late? It was after ten. Drying her hands as she went, she snatched her cell phone out of the pack's front pocket.

The ID screen only said Out of Area. Hoping it wasn't her mother trying to get hold of her, she answered tentatively. "Hello?"

"I know it's late." Mitch's baritone sounded short and strained. "I figured you'd still be babysitting."

"Yep, for probably another thirty minutes. You know, I'm still smiling. I had the best day."

"I know you did. Your eyes were shining."

"At first I thought I'd drown, what with all the near-death experiences."

"You didn't even come close to drowning. I wouldn't have let anything happen to you."

"I know. I had complete confidence in you. Otherwise I would have never let you drag me out into the middle of that river in the first place."

Yep, taking a chest full of shrapnel must feel just like this, Mitch thought. Deep, sharp cuts that exposed you clear to the heart. "We have new orders. We're leaving. I wanted to say good-bye."

"Wh-what? I thought you had another two weeks here."

The raw places in his chest seemed to throb, as fresh wounds did when air touched them. "Yeah. Orders change all the time. Believe me, this is not the way I want it, but in thirty minutes, I'll be on a bird out of here."

"Just like that?" In the background there was a faint scraping sound, like a wooden chair against linoleum. He pictured her clearly sitting down in that graceful way she moved and a crinkle digging in above her nose, the one he liked so much. Her voice became thin and concerned. "It's just so sudden. Is everything all right?"

"We lost a team and we're being brought in to replace them."

"That doesn't sound good. Y-you'll be coming back, r-right?"

He took a deep breath. *Please, Lord, help her to understand this.* He knew she had to be remembering how she'd lost Joe. "Believe me, I fully intend to come back. I've been doing this for a long time. I'm still here."

"But what you do sounds dangerous."

"I can't lie and say it isn't." He wanted to say this right, for Kelly's sake, ignoring the noise and bustle of his team packing up, all business. He was short on time. "We're well-trained and well-equipped. I know how to take care of myself and my team. You don't need to worry about me."

"Maybe I will anyway."

"No way. Put that energy toward something useful. Like acing your math final."

She didn't say anything.

That troubled him. She'd had a lot of people move in and out of her life. She still didn't trust him enough with those stories, but he could guess at what they were based on with what she'd already told him. In and out of foster care. Burying her fiancé. She'd known too much loss.

How did he make her see that he didn't plan on contributing to it? He didn't know. "No one can look ahead and see what's to come, but that's why we have faith, right?"

"Right. Faith is believing in things not seen. In trusting that the Lord will work things out for the good of His faithful."

"Exactly. So have a little faith, okay? In God. And it wouldn't hurt to have some in me, too."

"I already do." Her heart felt heavier with each breath. Her chest tighter. "Y-you have my e-mail address. If you get lonely over there, you're always welcome to drop me a note."

"I get awfully busy. I—" There was a lot of sound in the background. He came back on the line. "I've got to go. I just wish—"

Oh, she, too, wished that he didn't have to go. "Be safe, Mitch."

"I will. Goodbye, Kelly."

I can't take one more good-bye, Lord. There was no way she could make herself say more to him, so she disconnected and sat in the silence and shadows.

By the time the plane had leveled out, the city of Bozeman was nothing but tiny pinpricks of light tossed in the velvety night. Mitch pressed forward against the cold glass window, trying to keep the city in view. Kelly was down there somewhere.

I needed more time with her, Lord. It was tough to wrestle down his frustration. While he believed the Lord caused things to happen for a reason, what good could come of leaving her now?

I didn't have enough time to win her heart. It was like starting something he'd never have the chance of finishing. Like a loose end, unraveling. In another two weeks, maybe it would have been a different story. Now, he figured he might never know.

The city lights faded to black. The glacier crests of the Rockies below shone luminescent in the moonlight. Emptiness filled him like the wide endless stretch of the night. The gnawing feeling he'd left everything vital behind ate at him.

Kelly would be done with her babysitting job by now. She'd probably be heading home. She'd disconnected without saying good-bye.

That couldn't be a good sign. Not a good one, at all.

So many regrets. He disliked every single one of them.

Images of their afternoon together stuck in his mind. How she'd dazzled him when he'd pulled her up out of the water. He could still hear her laughter. How tender she'd made him feel. How right she'd been in his arms. The vanilla scent of her shampoo.

How could it be that the day wasn't yet over and he already missed her?

This might have been God's leading, but Mitch also knew with absolute certainty that she was his heart's choice.

In the well-lit apartment parking lot, Kelly locked her car door and glanced around the dark vehicles to make sure she was safe. The only movement was the shadows of the trees when the breeze rustled them. She sorted through the keys on the ring as she walked up the sidewalk. High overhead an airplane rumbled. It was a passenger jet from the local airport, not a military plane, but she thought of Mitch heading toward places unknown. Toward dangers unknown. And that made her feel as vulnerable as an exposed nerve.

There was no comfort in the hot, still night as she unlocked the front door and stepped into the darkness. Cool air blew over her as she crept into the kitchen, careful not to make a noise. Lexie was probably asleep by now, she thought as she opened the fridge and pulled out an orange soda.

But there was no comfort from the sugary drink. While the bubbles hissed and popped in the stillness, she curled up in the overstuffed chair in the living room where the moonlight and the glow from the streetlights fell through the window and onto her.

Mitch's words came back to her, rubbing on the exposed nerves in her heart. *I get awfully busy. I— I've got to go.*

In other words, she shouldn't count on him writing to her. She remembered his saying it was rare for him to have much free time. So, he was going to be way too busy to keep in touch. And, in time, too busy to remember her.

And if that made her sad, it wasn't like she was going to admit it. This was just as well—and how things were meant to be. The way she wanted it. She was keeping herself here on the riverbank of life. And she was afraid that if she reached out for those good, rare blessings she wanted, they would be whisked from her grasp.

Just like always.

Just like Joe had been.

Her devotional was in her backpack, and she dug it out. She couldn't remember the morning's passage—it had been such a long day. She felt a craving for the Scripture and flipped to the morning's text.

I teach you what is for your good, and lead you
on the way you should go.

She gazed out at the night stars. Mitch was out
there somewhere.

*Keep him safe, Lord. He's a good man. Please
give him a piece of the happiness You have in store
for me.*

It was all she had to give him. Mitch had his life,
she had hers. That was the way it was. But she would
always hold close the memories of their friendship.
She would always treasure the chance to have gotten
to know such a good man.

Chapter Nine

Kelly sat in a quiet corner of the campus cafeteria in the wash of the early-fall morning sunlight. Outside the sparkling windows other students hurried to their classes. She took a sip of coffee and turned the page of her sociology book.

Deep in the pocket of her backpack, her cell phone began to ring. Probably Amy calling to confirm—or to cancel—babysitting for a few nights this week. Kelly flipped open her phone. It wasn't Amy. She didn't recognize the number, but it wasn't a local one.

She answered it, and popping static filled her ear. "Hello?"

"Can you hear me okay?" asked a deep, familiar baritone that sounded very far away.

No, it couldn't be. "Mitch? Is that you?"

"The one and only. I'm just glad you remember me. It's been a while since I've talked to you."

How did she tell him that the days of September had slipped away like water down a drain, but he had been in her prayers every one of them. "You sound like you're calling from the moon."

"Just about. I feel like I'm in another world. There are no ice-cream cones here."

Oh, he sounded so good—so good and alive and strong...just like Mitch. She closed her eyes, and there he was in her mind's eye that day on the river. Standing waist-deep in water and grinning at her with a challenge. So larger than life and vital, looking as if nothing could hurt him. Of course, she knew that he was as vulnerable as anyone. "I can't believe it. I thought I'd never hear from you again."

"No way. You just try and get rid of me. I thought we were...friends."

"We are." The light in her heart brightened.

"I've got about ten minutes on this card. It has to be early there."

"It's twenty past seven in the morning, but I'm already on campus. Sitting in the cafeteria and trying to get some reading done before class. It's good to hear you. I've been—" Missing you. "—worried about you."

"Hey, I miss you. The guys I hang with aren't nearly as pleasing to the eye. How did the math final go?"

"I pulled an A. Thanks to you, but you don't want to hear about my classes."

"Sure I do. I put you in prayer every night. Even

when I'm out with my team doing things I can't tell you about, in places I can't tell you about either. Let's just say you're on my list, Kelly."

"L-list?"

Mitch's chest hitched painfully at the uncertainty in her voice. Nearly four weeks had passed since he'd left, and yet everything came back in a single heartbeat. The way her honey-blond hair gleamed. The dark-blue strands in her jeweled eyes. How her smile lit up his world.

She was the one. Thousands of miles away and continents apart, mighty affection crashed through him like a tsunami.

Whatever he did, he couldn't let her know. Not yet. The last thing he wanted to do was to scare her. He cleared his throat. "The list of the best things, to get me through. You know: ice-cream cones, riding the rapids, walking in the sunshine with a good friend."

"Right. That list." She sounded relieved, relaxed.

He was glad about that. They were friends now, but in time, he thought they could be more.

Her gentle alto warmed. "You're on my list, too."

"That means a lot. You can't guess how much." He didn't know how to tell her how tough the past weeks had been. It was a different planet where he was, or it seemed that way, where the phone bank was a luxury, and the fact that he'd had a lukewarm shower and hot chow for the first time in three weeks felt like a blessing. So were phone cards. His time was ticking away, and he hated that.

"When you called me before you left last month, you mentioned a team that was l-lost."

He squeezed his eyes shut, briefly, to hold everything in. "Yep. No one died. They were lucky, but there were serious casualties."

"Anyone you knew?"

"Yep. All of 'em. Don't worry. Those guys in 3rd Recon aren't as superior as my platoon."

She heard the catch in his voice. "I suppose you're invincible, huh, Mr. Action Figure?"

"Nope, just very careful. I intend to make it back home. You liked floating the rapids so much, I thought I might make good on my threat to take you mountain-climbing."

"I'm going to hold you to that threat."

His voice rumbled with reassurance. "Then we've got a deal. I'll be here in camp for a bit. They have us training pretty hard, but I'll be able to e-mail."

The line was crackling worse. "Mitch, I can barely hear you."

"Time's up. I've got to—"

There was a click and then nothing.

Be safe, she added silently as she disconnected.

The noise of the cafeteria was increasing around her as more students filed in for a quick breakfast. The tables nearby filled with students who gathered in groups to talk or sit quietly alone with their books and their coffee.

How come Mitch had such a hold on her heart? It took all her effort to turn her attention back to the work before her. She kept going over their conversation, over the sound of his voice. She kept picturing him, so handsome and capable in his camouflage clothing. Her heart gave a tug of admiration.

Careful, Kelly. No dreaming allowed.

Her phone rang again. Foolish seeds of hope sparked inside her, but it was Amy's number on the ID screen. Life went on as it should—with school, work and babysitting.

She knew better than to hope for more, but she sure wanted to.

Mitch hung up the phone. The hootch around him buzzed with pieces of conversations between other soldiers and loved ones at home, making him feel more alone than ever. Kelly was just so far away.

He tried to picture her in a campus cafeteria, probably lots of tables and chairs, noisy talking and the clatter of flatwear and dishes. She'd said she was reading, but was she studying? Or reading her devotional? He should have asked more questions to fill in the missing pieces.

She'd probably bought a cup of coffee, but anything else? A muffin? A breakfast sandwich? What was she wearing? It could get pretty cool in

Bozeman—probably a pair of jeans and one of those feminine cotton blouses she was always wearing. Maybe with a sweater. Was her hair pulled back in a ponytail with those little silken wisps curling around her face, or was it unbound, falling in a long sleek wave past her shoulders?

Not enough time. Not time on the phone and nowhere near enough time with her in Montana. When a man got down to it, there was never enough, not in a life, and he hated this feeling of regret. Of leaving things unfinished. His life had always been tidy, he liked things that way. It's what made him a good Force Recon marine. But the loose ends he'd left when he'd said good-bye to Kelly were ones he feared would unravel with distance.

There's not much I can do from here, he thought. His way of life was rugged and solitary, and there was no room for much else but his work. It would be simple just to let this go, whatever it was building between him and Kelly. That would be the safest route. That way he wasn't putting anything on the line. But he didn't want to move on from her, not deep down.

As uncertain as the path ahead was, he was committed. He was going to risk it all. She was far away, but he would do what he could.

He'd write her and he'd keep writing her until this tour was over and he was back on American soil.

* * *

While the noodles from her box of macaroni and cheese were boiling, Kelly set up her laptop on the dinette table in the eating nook and went online.

Should she be checking her e-mail? No. She had a ton of reading to do, but could she concentrate?

No way. Her conversation with Mitch had been on her mind all day. Of course.

Hearing his voice had done her heart good. Her day had been brighter as she hurried across campus from one class to another, took notes, grabbed a bite to eat on her way to her afternoon shift at the bookstore. Knowing that he hadn't forgotten her, that he still wanted to be friends, meant more than she wanted to admit to herself or to anyone.

She popped up from the table to give the noodles a stir—they were bubbling merrily on medium high—and then returned to study her screen. There was a new e-mail. Already? She couldn't believe her eyes. Her computer screen still looked the same—it wasn't her imagination. There really was an e-mail from Mitch. She opened it and started reading.

Kelly,
    No hand-dipped cones here. Chow hall pizza isn't half bad, except there are no cheesy sticks. But no complaining there. It's a step up from the meals in a can I get when we're out. Base camp is basically a lot of tents, but we've got heat most

of the time. I'm glad I got hold of you this morning. Good to hear a friendly voice from home. How did your classes go today? The next time you order pizza, eat a slice for me.
Mitch

The stove timer beeped a rhythmic electronic warning, dragging her away from Mitch's note. Already she felt happy as she drained the pasta, measured out the margarine and milk and stirred in the powdered cheese packet. Adding a generous sprinkling of pepper, she stirred until the cheese was warm and melted and dumped it onto a plate. On her way back to the laptop she grabbed a fork and sat down.

After a quick blessing over her food, she reread Mitch's e-mail, wondering what on earth to say back. He would probably be bored by her life; after all, he got to do all kinds of exciting things in a day. Her life was almost as boring as you could get.

She tried to picture living in a large camp of tents, but she could only imagine reruns of a seventies TV show that she'd watched over the years. Maybe it was something like that, sleep in one tent, shower in another, eat in another. If he'd mentioned the blessing of having heat that worked, then he had to be somewhere very cold.

She had no clue what to write. As she munched on her mac and cheese, she gazed out the window at the turning poplar leaves and the sunset blazing purple and magenta across the dome of the darkening sky. What would she say if he was standing in front of her?

Her heart stirred, and she started to type.

Mitch,

You don't know what it means to me that we can keep our friendship going when you're so far away. I get pretty wrapped up with studying—don't be shocked—I'm a little bit of a study-aholic, to use Lexie's term. Between trying to keep my A average and work enough hours to meet my monthly bills, I have about two hours left over in a week for a social life—which is mostly attending a weekly Bible study.

Lexie has been a blessing for a roommate because she tends to drag me places with her, like on Sunday afternoon. We went to the Museum of the Rockies with a couple of her friends and looked at fossils and Native American artifacts.

You're laughing, aren't you? Because that is *so* not a social life by most people's definition. The college group at church is having a singles' get-together at the town ice cream parlor next Friday night. Lexie has already told me she's meeting me after my shift at the bookstore and dragging me there. Should be fun.

Not only will I have a slice of pizza for you, but I'll make the sacrifice of eating a hand-dipped chocolate ice-cream cone for you, too. I'll suffer, sure, but friendship is worth it.

Blessings to you, and stay safe.

P.S. What kind of meals come in a can?

Kelly

As she polished off her meal, Kelly reread the e-mail, corrected spelling and sent it. It wasn't as if he'd have time to e-mail her for a while, but it felt good to write to him.

Maybe God had placed Mitch on her path because He knew how solitary her life had been since she'd buried Joe. Maybe He knew that Mitch needed a friend too, being so far from home and in danger.

She took comfort in that.

"Hey, I'm off to the library." Lexie burst out of her bedroom in a flurry. "Where did I put my card? I'm losing my mind. That's what I get for majoring in psychology. They say you gravitate toward what you need most, which is apparently therapy for me. Oh, now where did my keys go?"

"Over here." Kelly blinked to bring her eyes into focus, she'd been reading solidly for the past two hours. Night had fallen and the heat had kicked on. The weather was getting colder. She thought of Mitch and hoped that wherever he was, he was keeping warm. She grabbed the ring of keys on the coffee table by her mug of herbal tea and gave them a toss.

Lexie caught them. "Thanks. Oh, and I'd better

leave the rent check with you now, or I'll totally forget tomorrow. I've got it written out and everything." She pulled a check out of her pocket and dropped it on the counter. "I'll be back late. Anything you need while I'm out? Okay, I'm gone. See ya!"

Alone once again, Kelly tried to sink into her reading, but no such luck. In theory, her mind should be occupied enough with her studies to completely shove out every last thought of Mitch Dalton.

The practical aspect was a little different. Since she was never going to be able to concentrate properly unless she checked, she popped online while she microwaved another cup of apple cinnamon tea. Like he'd had time to answer her. No, not when she hadn't heard from him in a month. He'd already called, he'd already e-mailed.

She was not going to analyze the fact that she was hoping he'd answered. Apparently, Lexie wasn't the only one in need of therapy.

What she was not going to do was to check. She was going to go on to the library's Web site and do a little preliminary research for her next paper. Then, when she was done, she'd check her e-mail account.

The computer made an electronic bleep. An instant message popped on the screen from Mitchell Dalton. Kelly, got time to type at me?

The light inside her brightened another notch. She started to type.

For you, Mr. Action Figure, sure. I didn't know your extensive scouting skills included the ability to instant message.

She hit Send and waited. In a few moments, his answer popped on the screen.

I know a lot of stuff. So, what's this about a singles' meeting?

Now why would he ask that? she wondered. He was probably interested in the ice cream. She typed, You know the creamery shop downtown?

He answered in an instant. They have the best banana splits.

They do, she agreed. I usually get the chocolate fudge sundae, the one they sprinkle peanuts on top.

His answer shot back, You're killing me. I just had an unrecognizable casserole. It tasted like tuna and creamed potatoes.

Yum, she replied. It puts my mac and cheese to shame.

She left the message to post while she grabbed her steaming cup of water from the microwave. When she returned to the table, Mitch's answer was waiting for her.

You didn't elaborate on the singles' thing. You said you didn't date.

She shook her head in disbelief. Mitch had been blatantly clear about only wanting a friendship with her, as she'd been with him. She typed, It's not a date. It's a church group function.

A singles' function. His reply was almost instant.

I go for the ice cream and fellowship. I don't think I'll ever date again, she wrote.

Why not?

She stared at his question. The fragments of her past began to whisper behind the locked places in her heart. She wanted to silence those whispers, but her fingers were typing the words before she thought them.

Because I've stopped believing that good things are meant for me. She hit Send and waited, watching the cursor blink and feeling the beat of panic pulse through her. That was way too honest, but it was too late to take back the words.

Mitch's answer came immediately. I don't believe that. Not for a single nanosecond.

Old wounds ached like a sore tooth as she steeled her heart and wrote the plain truth. Life isn't a fairy tale—at least my life isn't. End of discussion. You never answered the question in the e-mail I sent. What kind of meals do you get in a can?

Nice try, came his answer, but I'm not gonna let you change the subject like that. What happened with Joe?

Her hands shook as she typed an answer. Two Saturdays ago I went to put flowers on Joe's grave. He's been gone three years now.

Maybe that was being way too honest—for herself and for poor Mitch who was just wanting to hear about the ice cream shop back home.

Then came his unexpected reply. I'm sorry. I know how painful it is to lose someone you care about. If it happens often enough, there comes a time when you can't stand to let anyone else too close. Not one more time.

He knew. Kelly squeezed her eyes shut to hold the emotions inside. How did she answer him? Anything honest she could say would hurt too much.

More words appeared on the screen. I've lost a few buddies over the years. Men I respected and thought of as my brothers. It's never easy to understand why. You had to have been devastated.

Yes, she typed and then stopped. Emotions she'd frozen in place and tucked away seemed to melt like icicles, and the drip of fresh pain made her want to push Mitch away and keep pushing.

The pieces of the truth she'd buried, that she hadn't shared with anyone, lay exposed.

She typed, I was devastated, but some wishes aren't meant to come true. You don't want to hear about that.

He answered, Sure I do.

Just find the words, Kelly. She dug down deep, and found the strength. Prayed for the ability to keep the tears out of her eyes and the sorrow from her heart. She should just tell Mitch, and then he would quit bringing it up. Besides, maybe it would be better for her to release the pain, write it down instead of saying the words out loud.

She began to type. Joe was working as a fire-fighter. You know the terrible forest fires we had in the national forests a few summers ago?

Yep, they made the national news. Even I read about them. Didn't a couple of fire fighters die over there? One of them was Joe?

She took a gulp of air as Mitch's question scraped against her exposed, open wounds. Yes, she answered. An unexpected high wind kicked up and trapped him and two other members of his team. This happened eight days before we were to be married.

She hung her head. She couldn't type another word. When she was finally steady enough to wipe at her burning eyes and face the screen, Mitch's answer was there, waiting patiently for her. You must have thought you'd finally had a real home. You lost everything with Joe. I'm sorry for that.

It wasn't meant to be, she typed and hit Send, feeling the shadows in the corners press against the light, against her.

She'd fallen so in love with the idea of being married and of being welcomed into such a warm and loving family. The little girl who'd always felt alone and adrift had finally come home to a husband and a kind extended family. It was her most heartfelt dream.

And to stand in the church sanctuary silent with hope and promises, and to plan, instead of a wedding, a funeral. To tuck away the dreamy wedding gown of silk and lace that Joe's sister had sewn for her and realize that this is how it would always be.

Mitch's answer flashed onto the screen. You're not alone.

How was it that he could know the words she most needed? She felt alone, at heart, at spirit, down to the soul. She knew God cared, that He watched over her, but not even her unerring faith could chase away the loneliness that clung with hungry talons and would not let go.

More of Mitch's reply scrolled across the screen. "Yet it was our weaknesses he carried; it was our sorrows that weighed him down."

She recognized the passage from Isaiah. Those words were a comfort that helped to chase away the memories lying as vulnerable as an exposed root:

memories of the little girl she'd been, the child with no stability or security, always wishing for someone to love her, just wanting to fit in, to belong to a real family.

The aftereffects of those memories left a bitter, cutting residue and her throat burned with unfelt emotions. She tried so hard to swallow them down, but they remained like a sticky mass, a tangle of feelings that she could not sort out. It took all of her effort to will the fragments of her past, of her memories, back into the locked room in her soul.

They typed at each other for another twenty minutes before he had to go. With training exercises awaiting him, he signed off, his heart heavy. He could feel the fragments of her broken dreams as sorely as if they were his own.

He missed her with a force so strong, he didn't want to examine it. But as he headed out into the bitter cold, and into the remote base camp of tents, not even the miles between them could break the connection he'd felt with Kelly.

His twisted-tight emotions roiling inside him began to unravel, thread by thread. He wanted to protect her. He wanted to comfort her. He wanted to make sure she was never alone. That she never hurt like that again. Overwhelming tenderness detonated like a cluster bomb, and he gritted his teeth as the explosion hit. There was no hiding from it. No denying it.

This love for her was as steady as an ocean's

current. As steadfast as the northern star. And twice as enduring.

It remained through the day of exercises and all through the night and into each long absorbing day of hard work.

It did not relent.

Chapter Ten

With the light of a new morning, Kelly had nothing but regrets. She'd stirred up feelings that she hadn't intended to. What troubled her most of all was that she trusted Mitch enough to tell him.

It had been easier, sure, since he was so far away, and she hadn't had to actually say the words out loud. But talking about her loss of Joe was one thing. Feeling Mitch's understanding was another.

He was beyond wonderful for having listened to her so politely, when he'd probably expected a much lighter electronic conversation. He'd been way too close, ironically, seeing as he was half a world away. Without seeing her, without so much as hearing her voice, he'd been able to crack her careful defenses. Defenses she hadn't realized were breachable until he'd walked into her life.

There was an e-mail from Mitch.

Kelly,

Glad you let me steal time out of your studies last night. I didn't really know Joe back in high school. You know he was a year older and ran with a different crowd, but he was a good guy. I am sorry for the grief you've gone through. We lost a team member this past year, he and I met at boot and we were buds. It was like losing a brother. Nothing is quite the same again—it isn't meant to be.

Hang in there. Write me when you get a chance. They keep you pretty busy here, but when you stop moving, you miss home and everyone there. I'm glad we're friends.

Mitch

Kelly took a sip of her coffee, warmed through by his words. Relieved, too. She put aside her cup and started to type.

Mitch,

Talking with you was the best possible study break. I was worried I'd been too personal last night. I'm used to keeping the real painful stuff private. It's just easier to deal with that way. The psychology classes I've taken say otherwise, but it works for me.

I know you've known loss, too. I am sorry about your friend. I imagine, when you eat, sleep, work and train together, that builds an immeasurably strong friendship.

I'm running late this morning, I should *not* be online but I was glad to see a note from you in my inbox and wanted to say thanks for listening. I'm pretty glad we're friends, too. I've got to go or I'm going to be stuck in the traditional 7:45 a.m. campus traffic jam.

Plus, then I'll get the farthest out parking spot and have a stitch in my side if I have to run to get to class on time. I have a policy on running, jogging or any kind of exercise—I am firmly against it.

Have a great day and stay safe.
Blessings, Kelly

Dear Kelly,

What? A no-exercise policy? That would never work for me. I have more of an exercise-only policy. I've been on the go since 0500 and it's after 2000. One hundred percent of my workday is physical. Did you make it to class on time? Inquiring minds wanna know.
Mitch

Dear Mitch,

I have a strict no-tardy policy to go along with my no-skipping-class policy. I'm sadly scholastically minded. I often sit in the front row, take copious notes and then study my notes that evening.

Scary, I know. I'm lucky my roommate still talks to me. She says I'm way too intense so that's why she hauls me to social events. There's an on-campus thing, Shakespeare in the Grass, that the drama department does, weather permitting. We're going to see *The Tempest* and then hit the pizza buffet. The play is free and there's a great student discount at the pizza place. So it's a night out that fits a student's budget perfectly.

Keeping you in prayer, Kelly

Hi there, Kelly,

Ice cream and pizza in the same week? See, I'm fishing for information. How did the singles' thing turn out?

Mitch

Dear Mitch,

I had a banana split with extra fudge sauce in your honor. Lexie and I got together with our friends Jessica and Rose. Sadly, the same guys keep coming to these events and no one is actually apparently going to date them, so the singles' thing is a misnomer. Plus, I am, like, three years older than any guy there, since I'm working my way through school so slowly. Jessica and Rose are coming to the play tomorrow, and because these guys overheard us talking, now the entire singles' group is coming. Stay tuned. I'll let you know if this blond perfect-looking dude that really likes Lexie actually talks her into dating. Lexie has a strict no-dating policy too. She thinks guys are untrustworthy.

Sincerely, Kelly

Dearest Kelly,
    Hey, I'm trustworthy.
Mitch, the most trustworthy guy ever.

Mitch,
    I never said you weren't. Lexie actually gave
you two thumbs up, a rare review. I think you won
her over with the cheesy sticks.
Blessings, Kelly

Hey, Kelly,
    What can I say? Buying cheesy sticks is always
the sign of a quality individual. I'm kidding, but
there's no way you can tell from here. I've never
seen a Shakespeare play. My impression is a stuffy
production where guys wear tights. Doesn't
sound dignified to me. I prefer something with a
lot more action. Hey, is watching Shakespeare
better outside or something?
Mitch, the uncultured

Mitch,
    You might be able to scale a glacier on a
mountain peak or know how to scuba dive and
you've probably done that sliding-down-the-rope
thing from helicopters, but you don't know excitement until you've experienced Shakespeare. There's
a lot of action. If you're ever in this neck of the woods
again, and school is in session, I'll drag you to one.

The play we went to this evening starts with a ship that wrecks at sea in a storm, and right when it was supposed to be raining in the play, it really did start to rain. There were cold storm gusts while the characters were getting blown around by the storm in the play. It was really cool, actually, but we were drenched. Lightning started up, and they had to call the production off due to the real tempest. We (the girls) hit the pizza place, stuffed ourselves with pizza and cheesy sticks and talked girl talk until about nine.

How did you spend your Saturday night?
Grace and peace, Kelly

Dearest Kelly,
Cleaning my gun. Then we had a rousing match of chess. I won every match except the championship of the night. It was a close call, but I fell in a brilliant move by Luke after an hour of battle. At least I went down with honor.

Cheesy sticks and pizza? I need details.
Take good care ok? Mitch

Dear Mitch,
We had our pick of every variety of pizza. I make it a policy to have a slice of each kind—the works, the meat supreme, the veggie, the Hawaiian, pepperoni, sausage and pepperoni. You name it. All but the cheese. The owner always

boxes up the leftover pizza when the buffet ends
and distributes it to the students. He's an alumni
and says he gets the student budget thing.

This is why we had cold pizza for breakfast. I
went for the straight pepperoni but Lexie prefers
the pepperoni and sausage mix for a higher
protein breakfast. And guess what we had for
lunch after church? You guessed it. Pizza. Enough
calories to see me through a long afternoon study
session. Do you get Sundays off?
I'm still keeping you in prayer, Kelly

Kelly,
Only in the sense that we're fragged for a
mission so this afternoon is prep. I'll be out of range
for a while, but I'll e-mail you when I get back. It's
rumored we may do that sliding-down-the-rope
thing from a helicopter that you mentioned before.
Thanks for your prayers, Mitch

Dearest Mitch,
I know, I have an amazing lack of military ver-
nacular. Keep your head down. Isn't that what they
always say in those old war movies? Stay safe.
Sending even more prayers, Kelly

Dearest Kelly,
Count on it. You're in my prayers too.
Mitch

* * *

Why did stat class always give her a headache? Because math was involved, that's why.

Kelly rubbed her forehead as she followed the stream of students searching for lunch. Noise from the lounge drifted into the busy corridor and Kelly picked up the concerned voice of a newscaster.

"Today, three marines were injured, when—"

The noise surged around her and drowned out the televised report.

She cut through the student traffic flow to the doorway of the lounge, where students sat with their lunch or books, listening to a cable news network. On the screen in the corner, she could make out a picture of a burning car in a desert-city street before the scene flashed on to other international news.

Mitch was in the mountains and not in the desert, so that news report wasn't in any way about him. But that didn't stop her fear or her worry for him. That was reasonable—he might think he was invincible, but he was wrong. He was not made of titanium.

The roar of the passing students drew her away from the lounge. She wanted to be able to find a table and the longer she stood in the hallway, the less likely that was going to be. She joined the herd moving toward the turnstiles at the cafeteria. The buzz of conversation, the clatter of trays and crunch of the ice machine echoed around her. It had been nearly five hours since Mitch's e-mail, and you'd think she'd stop thinking about him by now, but no.

There he was, front and center. What did she do about that? She cared about him, of course she did. He was a friend. A friend, nothing more, right?

As she grabbed a tray and maneuvered through the crowd toward the beverage dispensers, Mitch remained in her thoughts along with the strength of emotion she'd felt when they were online together. She missed him. It was that simple.

Not only had Mitch slipped beneath her defenses as if they were made of water, but he'd made her care about him. He'd made such an impression, he'd been such a good friend, that she missed having him present in her life.

It was certainly okay to care about a friend, so she shouldn't let it bother her that he was a male friend, right?

She grabbed a large cup and headed to the ice machine. She waited for the guy in front of her to finish. Her chest felt so torn apart, it hurt to breathe. Over the rattle of the ice and the sluice of lemonade into her cup, she tried to stop thinking. Tried to stop feeling.

She grabbed a container of strawberry yogurt and headed for the checkout lines. She chose the shortest one, but it was still a wait. As she inched toward the cashier, she didn't see an available table anywhere. Maybe she'd head outside and find a place in the shade, enjoy the last of the sunshine before it became too freezing to sit outside at all. Maybe she could get a start on her assigned reading. She had a huge paper due soon. *That* was what she should be thinking about—not a man God couldn't mean for her to have.

Mitch was far away preparing for a mission. She had no idea what that would be like, but it couldn't be easy or safe. She remembered how he'd mentioned tough nights sleeping in the elements, or creeping through enemy territory not knowing what waited ahead. How he'd said he needed a friend.

Well, that was what he was going to get.

Focus, man. Mitch crept forward with his team, silent and vigilant, weapon in hand. He heard something.

The clear thin air seemed to make the pre-dawn shadows look like liquid silver hugging the eastern side of the jagged mountain range. Bitter wind sliced across his face as he clenched his right fist and held it close to his chest. The team froze, sinking into the brush. His team members kneeled, facing outward, their backs to one another, defensive.

No sound. Nothing. That was troubling. He waited through long minutes until he heard it again. Mitch exhaled completely before speaking so his whisper would carry no real sound. "Someone's coming."

Every sense alert, reading the shadows, becoming part of the hillside, he waited. Mitch was confident whoever it was would pass on by without noticing his team. With any luck, they might get some scoop on the insurgent force in the area.

Low on the horizon the stars began to wink out as pale-gray light made the landscape stand out in black relief. The inky shadows turned from black to leaden gray, and dark purple brushed the high nearby peaks. Dawn was coming. They waited.

For one brief instant, a single thought pierced his concentration. Kelly. Half a world away, she was sound asleep, safe in her apartment.

The last stars faded as dawn came in its quiet glory. The light did not touch him as he remained motionless in the bitter cold, still waiting.

The cold autumn night temperatures nipped at Kelly's fingers as she fitted the deadbolt key into the door. Her ears were freezing, too, as she hadn't bothered with a hat or mittens for the short trek from the car to the apartment. Not her most brilliant move. What could she say? It had been a seriously busy week.

Shivering, Kelly let the storm blow her inside, fallen leaves raining down behind her as she closed and relocked the door. The air was chilly here too, although definitely not as cold as outside. She shrugged out of her coat.

"Sorry, I turned the heat on as soon as I got home," Lexie called from the kitchen. "But as I only got in about five minutes ago, it's still sixty-three degrees in here."

"What is that incredibly amazing aroma?"

"The upscale hot chocolate I love but can't really afford. My mom sent a care package today. Do you want chocolate raspberry, chocolate mint or chocolate hazelnut?"

"The raspberry one, please." Kelly dumped her backpack in the living room, where an opened cardboard box sat in the middle of the coffee table. All kinds of good things were exposed. "Your mom went all out."

"She wanted us to have good study food for midterms coming up. We'll be snacking off that for weeks. Hey, about an hour ago someone called for you." Lexie hit the timer on the microwave. "A certain handsome soldier."

"Mitch? He said he'd e-mail, not call. He's okay, right? He wasn't calling because he was hurt or anything?" She was talking way too fast. "I can't believe I missed his call. Why didn't he try me on my cell?"

"Oh no, he sounded perfectly macho and fine to me." Lexie leaned against the counter and smirked. "He was awfully eager to talk to you. In fact, when I told him you were working until eight, he said he'd call back between eight-thirty and nine. And guess what time it is right now?"

Kelly's gaze flew to the wall clock. "Eight twenty-nine."

He was going to call! Excitement at being able to

talk to him had her heading to her room. "If it rings, I'll answer the extension in here."

"I'm glad you and he are *just* friends."

Was that a hint of teasing she heard in Lexie's voice? But the electronic jangle of the phone made her forget Lexie's comment as she dashed the rest of the way down the hallway and into her room. She dove into her reading chair, snatched the receiver from its cradle and realized even as she said it, she was betraying her feelings way too much. "Mitch?"

"Yeah, it's me." His chuckle rumbled, wonderfully masculine and familiar, one of her very favorite sounds. "I'm glad I caught you. I thought for sure Lexie would answer and tell me that I didn't have to call at exactly eight twenty-nine."

Maybe she wasn't the only one who'd missed their friendship. That was nice, wasn't it? She leaned far enough, and stretched the cord so that she could nudge the door closed. "So, you're back all in one piece? No worse for the wear?"

"Well, I don't know about that. There isn't such a thing as a piece-of-cake mission, not on Force Recon, but it went like clockwork. Lasted longer than we thought. It's snowing where I am and hard enough that we're pulling snow-shoveling duty. I'm gonna need snowshoes just to get to the chow tent tonight."

"We haven't had a single flake here yet. What can you tell me about what you've been up to?"

"Not much, seeing as how it's classified, but I can say that I continue to win the best-cup-of-C-4-coffee honor in the team, twelve missions running. Luke thought he came close this time, but there's a talent to it he lacks."

"You're just naturally gifted, huh?" That made him laugh, warmed her heart, right down to her soul. "First I have to ask. What is C-4 coffee?"

"It sounds like extra-explosive caffeine, doesn't it? Nah, we can't have a fire to cook on, the smoke would definitely give us away, thereby ruining the stealth aspect of our mission. So we light teaspoon hunks of C-4 on fire and cook over the flame. It takes a lot of practice to make that perfect cup of morning coffee."

"You're kidding me, aren't you? You can't cook with explosives. Can you? It doesn't sound sane."

"Now I never said I was sane." That made him laugh. "I'm telling you the truth. It's how we heat our cans out of our MREs, Meals Ready to Eat. It makes whatever is inside the can—no one can tell for sure—taste almost edible. But when you're hungry enough, you don't really care."

"That's why you were so interested in my pizza when we were instant messaging."

"There's a lot of things I miss when I'm over here." Pizza was the least of those things. She'd gone right to the top of his most-missed list. After spending the last two months hunting down terrorists, a physically and mentally tough duty, being able to hear the goodness of her voice was a true luxury. "I'm already running out of things for my warm-thoughts list."

"That sounds serious."

"Yep, I don't want to be forced to head out on my next mission with a diminished list."

"Wow, that would border on a crisis." The smile was in her voice.

Mitch's chest twisted tight. "Help me out, would ya? You could send me suggestions in e-mail. That way I could fortify my puny list with all kinds of real-life details."

"Trust me, my real life isn't all that splendid."

"Hey, I think so. Besides, I had a long list prepared, and I've gone through it already."

"It must be pretty rough and pretty cold where you are right now. You know I'd be happy to do anything I can for you. Be-because you're such a good friend."

He loved that hitch of emotion in her voice. Yeah, he thought, he had the same problem. He was starting to care way too much for safety's sake. And that was all right with him.

"Friends ought to help each other when they can." Her heart was in her voice.

He liked that. "I'd like to hear about all the good things in your life that shouldn't be taken for granted. For instance, the heat in your apartment."

"It's a lovely thing. You turn on the thermostat and the place warms right up. So, are you sure you want to hear about all the warm blessings in my life? I'll probably bore you."

"Not a chance." Caring like this was nice, but it was also a little like watching a grenade roll toward him, closer and closer, about to go off and there was nowhere to escape. All he could do was brace himself for it to blow.

"Then I'll send you an e-mail every day and tell you about the good things in my life, if you do the same."

"I'll be scarce, but when I'm in, I'll send you my daily compilation. How's that?"

"Perfect."

Yep, that pretty much described how he felt, too.

As they talked through the two hours of his calling card, he couldn't help feeling they became closer with each passing minute. It was nice. Real nice.

Chapter Eleven

It was seriously late, nearly midnight on a Friday night, and they'd been slammed at the bookstore, and closed up nearly an hour later than usual. But Kelly wasn't about to renege on her promise to Mitch.

As her laptop dialed in, she tiptoed around the kitchen and grabbed an orange soda from the fridge and a bag of iced animal cookies Lexie's mom had sent. There was a sticky note on the bag that read, "Kel, eat these please, before I go up another pant size."

Misery loves company, apparently, or at least the diet-challenged. While she munched on an iced elephant, she checked her inbox. There was an e-mail from Mitch.

Dearest Kelly,
    Hiya. Here's my list from today. One. Never

take a small snowfall for granted. When twelve inches falls in a twelve-hour period, you learn what else to never take for granted.

Two. Your back remaining pain-free and limber.

Three. Food you recognize. They said it was taco-seasoned hamburger, but we were skeptical, as the refried beans looked the same.

Four. Never take for granted sleeping through the night.

What's your list?

Keeping you in prayer, Mitch

That man sure could make her smile. Kelly sipped her soda and sat at the table, trying to stop the memories of their talk last night. He'd had her laughing for nearly an hour solid. He'd said nothing notable, he was simply being Mitch, and she loved his sense of humor.

He made her feel as if she'd been filled with stardust. Even now it was a wonder she didn't glow like the Milky Way.

She started typing.

Mitch,

First on my list. Iced animal cookies. Not great for your warm-things list, but they go perfectly with any hot drink. Coffee. Tea. Cocoa.

Second. Sunshine on your face. It was a perfect late-autumn day today. You know how the mid-afternoon sun gets toasty warm, even though there's a chill in the wind? The air smells woody and morning frost smelled like winter. And all day long there's the crisp crackly frost on the ground.

How am I doing?

Third. The quiet right before midnight. When you've had a long hard day, and you sit in the shadows and let the peace settle around you. There's a half moon mid-zenith, shining as orange-yellow as a harvest moon. It makes the glacier caps on the mountains shimmer like opals. It's the perfect time for praying. It feels as if the angels are leaning over, listening extra hard.

Tonight, when I say my prayers, I'll put you in them. Be safe.

Your friend, Kelly

Kelly hit Send. And because it *did* feel as if the angels were waiting, she bowed her head and prayed from her heart.

While racking a round into the chamber of his weapon in the base camp's firing pit, Mitch felt a strange tug in his chest. Not like a kick of adrenaline, but this was a slow steady burn like a star winking to life in a twilight sky.

A snowflake brushed his cheek and as he cradled the familiar weight of the MP-5 in both hands, he knew that back home, Kelly was awake and thinking of him.

This relationship thing was still like driving in the dark, but at least he wasn't alone.

Dear Mitch,

Hi. The list of good things continues: Fellowship. The college group at church. We're too old for youth group and too young for the women's groups, the women there are married, and if not, then they are at least adults with real lives. College is that sort of in-between place. So we stick together, firmly bound by worries over our studies, grades, professors and what-are-we-going-to-do-when-we-grow-up kind of things. We had volunteered to help with the autumn harvest festival, which we have for the kids' Sunday-school groups on Halloween, so the kids have a good place to go for that evening. Our group is making the candy bags.

So, picture about twenty college kids sitting around the multi-purpose room talking and stuffing gallon-sized zipper bags with miniature packages of M&Ms and little Snickers and, my personal favorite, Whoppers. Sadly, some of the candy never made it into the bags. Needless to say, we were all extremely sugar-buzzed by suppertime and had to go out and buy more candy to replace what we'd consumed.

I'll keep you in prayer. Stay safe.
Kelly

Dear Kelly,

Hey, I love Snickers and candy corn. I once ate an entire pound bag of them, and Mom had the biggest conniption. I was six, and after zipping around the house full-speed for thirty minutes, I

got seriously sick. I learned my lesson. Sadly, I had many such lessons to learn as a little kid.
Mitch

Dear Mitch,
   You? I find that hard to believe.
Blessings, Kelly

My Dear Kelly,
   Believe it. The most memorable lesson was the coronary I gave my mom when I was four. I climbed the rock wall of the living-room fireplace to the top—all two stories. My little sweaty hand-print is still on the cathedral ceiling. I can still hear Mom, over twenty years later, scolding, "Mitchell James Dalton, *what are you doing?* You get down here right this minute!"
Sending prayers, Mitchell James Dalton

Dear Mitchell James Dalton,
   So, you're telling me you were trouble right from the start? And your poor mom. She didn't deserve that.
Kelly

Dearest Kelly,
   That's what she says, too. But I always tell her the apple doesn't fall far from the tree.
Mitch

* * *

Shivering from the morning cold, Kelly slid into her usual chair in the middle of the auditorium classroom, balanced her to-go cup of coffee on the desktop and lowered her backpack to the floor at her feet.

A glance at the clock over the door told her she had fifteen minutes before class started. Perfect! She'd had such a great time e-mailing back and forth with Mitch over the last few weeks, that she'd been collecting ideas for her list on the walk to campus.

She set her laptop on the desk and started a letter to send later, when she was on break at work.

My Dear Friend Mitch,

Eggnog lattes. I had the very first one of the season from the coffee shop at the corner of campus. Sweet creamy eggnog meets hot soothing coffee. Whoever invented this drink is a certifiable genius. It's perfect on a crisp November morning to warm you clear through, which leads me to the next thing on my list.

Frosty wintry mornings, the kind where white frost has settled everywhere and on everything—tree branches, crisp fallen leaves, car windshields, and it glitters when the sun hits it. Little waves of evaporation rise up from the early-morning streets, and the blades of grass crunch beneath your shoes. The cold burns your face and your breath rises in cloud-like puffs. There's a peaceful joy to walking to your first class on a morning like this—with an eggnog latte.

Kelly paused over the keyboard. It was an odd thing, how different she felt whenever she was thinking about Mitch, or writing to him, or simply hearing his voice. The shadows and difficult memories she hid behind lock and key faded away, and her heart felt whole.

A movement over the top of the screen caught her attention. It was Lexie, on her way to her class down the hall. She dropped into the empty seat next to Kelly. "Hey, roomie. You look studious. Oh, a letter to that soldier of yours. Nice."

"He's not mine. You know that."

"Sure. Just friends. I get it." Lexie rolled her eyes, good-naturedly. "Hey, I saw the note you left on the message board. I'm in. What time do you want a shopping buddy? And what are we shopping for?"

"Your mom's care package inspired me. I want to send something like that to Mitch."

"Great idea. Where is he stationed, do you know?"

"He only said it was a remote base camp, but I think the location is classified."

"Cool. I've never known anyone before who was classified. Ooh, I'll think of a list of stuff while I'm trying not to fall asleep in class. Which I've gotta get to. Adios." She rose, hoisting her backpack onto her shoulder. "How about in front of the library, around eleven?"

"See ya there." One glance at the clock and the students streaming through the doorway told her that she didn't have time to write anymore.

But she was going to start a list of her own, too. He was going to get the most fun care package ever. She hated to think of all the hardships he lived with every day. By choice and by duty, she understood that, but still. It was a sacrifice to be so far from home, and she owed him a little happiness in return for what his friendship had given her.

Just when she'd thought her heart would be as if in shadows forever, Mitch had come along and unknowingly made her feel joy again.

Yep, wherever he was, whatever he was doing, she owed him. Big-time.

The medevac's *whop-whop* faded into the silence of the high-mountain Afghan night and Mitch gave one last thought homeward as he moved out with his now three-man team. Luke had been shot during their ambush.

Not good. His team hadn't been standing still for more than a couple of minutes while they'd loaded up Luke, but already they were all shivering.

"Pick up the pace." They had to put in as much distance as they could as quickly as they could, because the helicopter was like a flashing neon sign to the terrorists, hey, look over here.

At least the storm blowing in would eventually

cover their tracks. They had a long hard walk through thigh-deep snow. There was nothing like a fast hike with their packs on their backs to get the blood pumping again.

Kelly. There she was, like a steady candle's flame burning intractably against the dark. Right in his heart, and that light did not fade even as his every thought and his entire focus was on staying alive and completing his mission.

By the time this was over, he was going to forget what warm felt like. But he knew that light would still be burning.

The first frozen pellets of snow tapped off his shoulders. Yeah, it was gonna be a tough night.

With fifteen minutes to spare, Kelly pulled into a spot in the employees' parking behind the store and slid to a careful stop. Gray skies spat freezing drizzle, and a fine coating of ice gleamed on everything.

But did she care? Nope. Her boots skidded as she stood, but she managed to keep her balance as she grabbed her backpack and the huge shopping bag full of Mitch's stuff from behind the seat. It was heavy— she and Lexie had totally blown her budget—but she couldn't wait for him to see all this.

Happiness filled her up and she hardly noticed the drip of ice against the back of her neck as she struggled past the door and into the warmth of the building.

"I'm glad you made it in one piece. It's horrible out there." Katherine looked up from her book, propped open on the lunchroom table before her. She looked elegant, as always, in a slim black blouse and skirt, and her eyes lit up with interest over the bag. "Hey, you've been shopping. Did you get anything good?"

"Lots of stuff, but not for me." She dumped her pack on the floor by the employee closet and set the bag on a corner of the table. "Would you mind if I used one of the empty boxes from yesterday's shipment? I'm sending this to a friend."

"Sure. This wouldn't happen to be for your marine, would it?"

"Oh, he's not my marine." Just saying that aloud made her feel…strange.

"You mean you aren't staying in touch with him?" Katherine peeked into the bag. "We're talking about that drop-dead gorgeous guy with the shoulders of steel, right?"

"That would be the one. We're e-mailing now and then. And he called me."

"Good." Katherine seemed sedate as she rifled through the bag, but there was a subtle glint in her eye.

Kelly didn't miss it or the meaning behind it as she removed her coat. "He's just a friend."

"Right. Of course he is." Katherine didn't look convinced. "Where is he stationed?"

"He's overseas at a base camp. I'm guessing in Afghanistan or somewhere close to there. He said he couldn't say. He's on something called Force Recon."

"Oh, I know what that is. I used to be engaged to a guy whose brother was a Force Recon marine. Those are the real stealthy guys. I know Trevor did everything from deep-ground reconnaissance to counterterrorism. The training is more extensive than for the SEALS, I think. That's like, wow."

Kelly was starting to have the same opinion about the man. "That would be Mitch."

Katherine marked her page and put her book aside. "You know, we don't have a single customer. The weather is keeping everyone away. Why don't we start going through the store? I'm sure there a few things we can find that your marine would like. Some of the Christmas shipments have started to come in, and there's a lot of fun stuff. C'mon."

"He's not my marine." Why did the pieces of her lost dreams seem to ache when she said that? But Katherine apparently wasn't listening, she'd already swept out of the room.

Katherine was right, there was a lot of good stuff. As they sorted through the boxes waiting to be inventoried and shelved, Kelly couldn't get her mind off her boss's words. *Your marine,* she'd called Mitch.

It was really strange, because Lexie had called him *that soldier of yours* earlier this morning. It was like a clue from heaven—except that was totally not possible. No way. It wasn't what she wanted; it wasn't what Mitch wanted. Not rationally, anyway.

But, in truth, her heart longed for more than friendship. The little girl inside her, always alone and wanting to belong, longed, too.

If only there was a way he *could* be my marine, she thought. It was a wish that came from her heart, where she could not afford to start wishing. Only pain came from that.

She'd lost enough. Mitch was her friend. When he was done with his tour of duty and stationed in California, which he called home, he wouldn't be needing a friend. He wouldn't be needing her.

It was best to be practical. It was the only way to protect her heart. She was alone.

And that was how it was meant to be.

But as she sorted through the new stock, which would be perfect for stocking stuffers or a care package, she couldn't help the smallest hope in her heart that wherever he was, he was safe. And, did she dare hope that he was remembering her?

If he'd had a more miserable night, Mitch didn't want to think about it. His turn at watch was over and as he huddled into his sleeping bag and stared at the tarp tied overhead to keep off the falling snow, he shivered hard. Now, if he could only warm up enough to fall asleep, he'd be happy.

Not so easy. The frigid chill from the permafrost

he'd bedded down on seeped through the bottom layer of the sleeping bag. He let his mind wander to that summer afternoon with Kelly. It had been hot that day, so hot it warmed to the bones. He tried to remember how that felt, the warm lush green grass, the sunshine so hot and bright it sizzled across the river water onto his skin, but he couldn't visualize it. The images remained in the background, kind of fuzzy and distant.

What he remembered, as clearly as if he were in Montana right now, was Kelly. The rippling sound of her laughter when he'd scooped her out of the river. How good it had felt to have her at his side as they'd walked through the park. She'd looked pretty as could be in the university T-shirt and denim cut-offs she'd worn, and her sneakers had squeaked in the grass, still damp from the river.

He remembered how the sunlight had brushed her with bronze, making her blond hair blow loose ripples and shine like gold. How she'd eaten her dipped cone by peeling off the thick chocolate layer first, eating it in dainty bites.

He tried to imagine her right now, using what she'd told him about her life. Her morning classes would be over. She'd probably be starting her shift at the bookstore. Maybe she'd have an eggnog latte to keep her warm, and she'd be ringing up sales in the store, chatting with the regular customers, or bowed over one of her schoolbooks during the lulls.

While he thought of her, the misery of the frigid cold and the hard day's exhaustion released its hold on him and he slept.

Chapter Twelve

The low squeak of a door startled Kelly out of her thoughts. She looked up from the final printed draft of her research paper. She'd been concentrating so hard, she was surprised to see the gray light of dawn sneaking around the closed blinds and her roommate stumbling in her robe and slippers toward the bathroom.

"How long have you been up?" Lexie asked on a big yawn.

"Since five. I keeled over about one and thought I'd get up early and get this proofed and printed before I left this morning. Ha." At least, it had seemed reasonable in the wee hours of the morning, but in the light of day, not so much. "Not as easy as I thought."

"Tough. I'll be you next week. I've *got* to start the paper that's due." Lexie wandered into the bathroom, yawning.

It was contagious. Kelly stifled a yawn as she

spotted a typo and turned to the computer to correct it. The printer she'd set up on the corner of the table whirred and spat out the corrected page. She forged ahead with her reading.

Time kept ticking past and when finally she was satisfied with her printed copy, Lexie was out of the bathroom, hair wrapped in a towel and grabbing a container of yogurt from the fridge. "Kelly, you need any help?"

"No. Ta-da! I'm done." With not a second to spare. She had just enough time to grab a quick shower, pack up and race out the door.

It didn't occur to her until she was bundled up and scraping the thick sheet of ice off her windshield, that she'd forgotten to check her e-mail. Well, it was too late now. She'd faithfully sent an e-mail every day, and she hadn't gotten a response since she'd shipped off the package last week. She'd spent the last six days trying not to think of him. And she'd failed.

And now here she was thinking of him again and feeling confused and turned upside down and vulnerable all at once.

She missed him. As a friend, right?

But, as she circled around to the rear window and began to chip away at the stubborn sheet of ice, she was no longer sure.

No answer.

Mitch swiped his hand over his face. Disappointment hit him like a brick. He'd thought for sure there would be another day's e-mail, sent like all the others. But for some reason she'd skipped the last two days, and now this morning.

Why? Lord, I'm too far away. You gotta help me here, I'm begging. Don't let her start drifting away. Considering his current altitude, he was closer to heaven, but Mitch didn't get a sense that God was hearing him any better for it.

He felt lost as he sent his e-mail. Kelly and her world of brightness and sweetness, of eggnog lattes and studying and college-life groups no longer seemed real at all. One of his best friends had been evacuated to a hospital, and while they'd succeeded in their ambush, they had paid a price.

He'd reread her e-mails, he'd saved every one, listing all the good things in her daily life. But even reading her words didn't make him feel as connected to her as he once had. He wanted to hear her voice. He needed to hear it. But, when he counted ahead to calculate her time, it was about eight o'clock in the morning. She'd probably be seated in her first class, bright-eyed and ready to take copious notes.

He bit back the frustration. He'd try her later, after he hit the rack and got some much-needed sleep. Maybe she would have found his e-mail by then and responded.

"I guess our Christmas rush has officially started." Katherine sounded exhausted as she locked up her till. "I'm going to take my lunch now that we seem to have quieted down for a moment. I'll be in the back. Page me if you get overrun, okay?"

"Are you kidding? It's two o'clock and you've been running since well before I got here." Kelly looked up from where she knelt before the point of purchase displays near the front counter. "You just go put your feet up, get something to eat and relax. You deserve it. Whatever happens up here, I can handle it for a bit. Ava should be coming in any time to help out."

"Yeah. Send that sister of mine back when she gets here, all right?" Katherine grabbed her book from beneath the counter and tapped away in her heels.

Kelly kept stocking. While the sound system played instrumental hymns, she replenished the bookmark display, moving just as fast as she could. The coupons Spence had printed in several of the local church papers had brought in more business than they'd expected. And she still had the card section to get back up to snuff before the next wave of customers hit.

It looked as though there wouldn't be much of a chance to study from here on out. Or, she thought sadly, a chance to log onto her account, using her laptop in the break room, to check her e-mail. Not that Mitch was likely to answer. He was probably busy climbing mountains, rappelling from helicopters, practicing his marksmanship and saving the world. He had important things to do, and she was only a friend. Like a pen pal. Which is exactly what she'd wanted all along. So exactly why did that hurt? Why was she swallowing down a wave of disappointment?

Whatever happened, she could not give in to hoping. Not even a little. So she sent a gentle *friendly* prayer his way.

She would simply have to accept that it was only natural that he would start to drift away. Their friendship was only temporary. He was partway through his tour of duty. By sometime in December, he would be back at his home base in California and he wouldn't need a pen pal after that.

No. She had to simply deal with the fact that as much as she respected Mitch and as much as she liked him, he wasn't hers to keep. As a friend or otherwise. Their lives had gone separate ways and that's how it was meant to be.

She'd known that all along. Mitch would be just another person in her life she would have to say good-bye to. But if she was smart, she could keep him from getting too close. That way, she could be sure that when he did say good-bye for good, he wouldn't be taking a piece of her heart.

It sounded logical, like a good plan. Except the thought of losing Mitch—even as a friend—cracked her heart a little more deeply.

Too late, she thought as she stood, taking the empty boxes with her.

* * *

Mitch was glad to be back at camp. He wasn't glad that it was 0500 and he was freezing, but he tried checking e-mail anyway.

No go. No phones with the current storm. They were under whiteout conditions. When they'd be up was anyone's guess. He might as well be based out in the northern tundra for all the good these gadgets were doing him.

Frustration ate at him like the gnawing cold. The heater had conked out again and couldn't keep up with the subzero temps. And he couldn't keep up with his growing frustration.

"C'mon, Dalton." Pierce poked his head in. "We've got PT in five."

"Yeah, I know."

Mitch stood, biting down his frustration. Physical training was just what he needed. It would give him something to focus on. He'd be able to shove out these tangled emotions and struggle with something that was concrete and easier to overcome. He would push harder and harder until every problem and every feeling faded into nothing.

At least, that was the theory. But as he turned his thoughts to the workday ahead, he suspected that all the ways he missed Kelly would remain.

No matter what.

Kelly stumbled through her front door a few minutes after eight-thirty. Her veins were still pulsing adrenaline from her icy drive home. "I can't believe I made it in one piece."

"Whew, I'm glad to see you." Lexie looked up from the couch, where a thick text was open on her lap. The TV droned, volume low, in the background. She capped her highlighter. "There was an emergency broadcast on the road conditions. I'm glad they sent you home early."

"Spence closed the store when we lost power, half the town is out, but it took me forty minutes to drive three miles." She hung up her coat and carted her backpack and computer case into the warm kitchen.

Finally, she thought as she unzipped her laptop. She'd pop online, send her daily list and maybe there'd be a letter from Mitch. And if there wasn't…well, she refused to be disappointed.

But before she could find the phone cord to plug into her computer, the lights blinked. The TV silenced. Darkness washed over them.

"No fears," Lexie said from the pitch-black living room. "I've got a flashlight here *somewhere*."

There was rustling, the sound of something hitting the floor, and a round beam of light came to life, highlighting Lexie's smile. "I was prepared. With the ice storm and winds, I figured we had a good chance of losing power."

"I can still dial in if there's a dial tone." She checked the line. Yes! It was working. She connected the phone cord and dialed in quickly, before she lost that, too.

"I'll light candles," Lexie said as she rescued the remote control from the floor. "You check for love letters from Mitch."

"They aren't love letters, trust me. Why does everyone have the same misconception?" Kelly knew it irritated her for only one reason—a tiny part of her was wishing for love. And how crazy was that? Insane. Certifiable. She knew better, too. Whatever it took, she would *only* allow friendship-type thoughts and feelings about Mitch.

And that was that.

There was an e-mail from Mitch waiting for her. She couldn't believe it. She had to blink twice just to make sure. His name really was there. He was safe, and he hadn't forgotten her *yet*.

She could hardly breathe past the joy filling her as she downloaded the document before the phone went out too. Lexie circled around the counter and set a pillar candle on the table. Kelly looked up. "I should get up and help you."

Lexie grinned knowingly. "You should answer Mitch. I take it he wrote?"

"Yeah," she cleared her throat, trying to sound blasé. "I guess he had time to write or something."

Lexie lit a match and set it to the wick. Just as blasé, she said, "Then I guess you should answer him or something."

"Maybe." Kelly didn't want to admit it, but everything within her yearned for the sight of his words.

This was more than simple friendship, a tiny voice at the back of her mind warned her, but she refused to listen. She was already opening the document, devouring his letter.

Dearest Kelly,

I know, I'm finally getting back to you. Hey, your lists are great. You don't know what it means to come in after being out for over a week, and have so many e-mails waiting for me. Here's my list of things:

1. I'll never take a Saturday afternoon relaxing on the couch for granted. I especially miss this luxury after hiking with my team ten clicks with a fifty-pound pack on my back in a high-mountain blizzard.

2. Not having to watch your best buddy get shot.

3. Being warm enough to feel your hands and feet at all times.

4. Going to sleep without having first to set up claymore mines and sensors. Each man takes turns at keeping watch, but deep sleep is impossible. You're always listening for the sound of one of the mines going off, meaning your armed enemy is close while you're still in your sleeping bag.

5. Sleeping in a warm place instead of being too cold to fall asleep.

6. Life is uncertain. Never take your friends for granted.

I'll give you a call as soon as I can.

In prayer, Mitch

Wow. Kelly's jaw dropped. She couldn't imagine what Mitch had been through. She reread his words and felt sorrow for his suffering.

"What's wrong?" Lexie turned from lighting a pillar candle on the counter. Light flickered eerily as she hurried over. "Mitch is okay, isn't he?"

"I guess." What did okay mean? She didn't know. "Read this and tell me what you think."

"Mitch won't mind?"

"No, we're really just friends, and he's writing nothing that's private." At least, she didn't think so. Mostly, she couldn't quite believe what her eyes told her, and her heart didn't want to feel. She'd seen enough war movies to be able to fill in the blanks in all that he hadn't said with images of her own. "What do you think?" she asked when Lexie finished reading over her shoulder.

"I'll tell you when my jaw stops dropping. What does Mitch do, anyway? Is he Special Forces?"

"Yeah." Kelly didn't want to get online to answer him. What if he tried calling? He'd get a busy signal. "I hope his friend is all right."

"Me, too. That puts my day in perspective." Lexie pulled out a chair and sat down. "I'm really glad you sent him that care package. He probably hasn't gotten it yet?"

"Doesn't sound like it." Kelly shrugged, wishing she could do more. So much more. Then she realized it was late where he was. In the wee hours of the morning in his part of the world. He wouldn't be calling, so she tried to get back online, but the modem couldn't get a dial tone.

Just as well. She was no longer a child to believe in fairy tales, but it was nice to know there were good guys in the real world. Very nice.

She shut down her computer and got right to her studies, but her thoughts kept drifting to him. To the radiance he brought to her soul, like starlight on a frosty winter's night.

Mitch shivered in the freezing-cold tent and hooked the receiver between his ear and shoulder. While he dialed the last digits of Kelly's home number, he knew chances were good that she wasn't home. She had probably headed straight to work after her morning classes.

As he listened to the first ring and then the second, he figured he'd at least leave a message on her answering machine. He wouldn't try her cell, not when she'd probably be at work.

Sure enough, a recorded message answered. "This is Kelly," came her voice as sweet as the dawn. "And

Lexie," Lexie added. "We're away right now," and Kelly's soft alto piped in, "so please leave a message!"

He waited for the beep. "Hey, Kelly, it's Mitch. I'm bummed that I missed ya. I'll try back."

He hung up, the numbers on his watch showing it was four minutes past four in the morning. He'd gotten up early just to try calling her.

Well, there was nothing to do but to keep at it. He wouldn't stop calling until he reached her. Until he could hear her voice, all heart and goodness, because he needed some of that.

He needed her.

In the silence of Amy's living room, Kelly snapped her book shut, the sound as startling as a gunshot in the sleeping house. The kids were asleep. The scents of crayons and SpaghettiOs lingered pleasantly in the air. With the fire crackling in the hearth, she should feel peaceful. It was a perfect studying climate. But could she concentrate? No.

Lexie had called about an hour ago, while she was clearing supper dishes from the table, to tell her that Mitch had called and left a message. Ever since, she'd been keeping her silent cell phone close just in case Mitch tried again.

She resisted the urge to hop online and check her e-mail account. That would make it obvious, even to herself, how eager she was to hear from Mitch. And if she was going to hold tight to her stance and to her vow to keep her feet on the ground when it came to Mitch, then she couldn't go around acting as if she wanted to fall in love with him, right?

Right.

The living-room walls felt as if they were pressing in on her until she couldn't draw a single breath. She wanted to blame it on studying too hard, but she *always* studied hard. That was no excuse. The real explanation was something she didn't want to think about.

And somehow, she had to make sure she stopped thinking about Mitch and kept every thought of him from her mind. Maybe it was better that he hadn't called. Maybe this was a sign, this pattern of missed communications. Maybe, she thought desperately and with hope, it was a sign from above reminding her she was looking down the wrong fork in the road.

Her cell phone rang. Surely that wasn't a sign, either. She checked the screen—an out of area number. Mitch, her heart hoped wildly before her common sense kicked in and she let it ring a second time. Then a third.

Now she was *definitely* in need of therapy. First she couldn't wait for him to call and now that he probably was, she didn't want to answer the phone. For some reason it felt like a monumental decision as she pressed the button to accept the call, which made no sense at all. At the back of her mind, she worried this could be her mom calling, too. "Hello?"

"K-Kelly." Above the crackle of static in the long-distance line, she heard his voice.

"Mitch." His name was on her lips, as if straight from her heart, and her voice betrayed her. Joy blazed within her. She hadn't realized until this moment how much she'd missed him. How much she'd worried over him. His voice might be her most favorite sound on earth. "I can't believe it. It's really you."

"No imposter this time. You're a difficult lady to get a hold of lately."

"Not as difficult as you are, mister. Are you okay?"

"Right as rain, or maybe I should say snow this time of year. Are you all right? When you answered, you sounded like were hesitant to talk to me. You're not at work, are you? It's okay that I'm calling?"

Please, let it be okay. Mitch gripped the phone tightly.

"Y-yeah, it's absolutely okay, I'm just babysitting. It's just that your number came through as 'out of area' and with an area code I didn't recognize. I was afraid it was my mom using a calling card from jail."

"She does that a lot?"

"No, I'm just always cautious. But you didn't call to hear about that. How is your friend doing?" There was her heart, unmistakable in the warm tones of her voice.

Man, it was good to hear. His chest twisted tight, so strong it was a physical pain that came from missing her. "Haven't heard about Luke yet. He's been flown to a hospital in Germany."

"He must have been hurt pretty badly."

"Y-yeah." He cleared his throat. He'd save thinking about what had happened, seeing his friend shot and defending him while their corpsman worked frantically to save his life, along with the rest of them. Their ambush on the enemy had been a success, and their mission was completed—but at a personal cost. As always. "All we can do is wait. And pray."

"I've been keeping him in my prayers, and Lexie has, too. I let her read your e-mail. Was that all right?"

"Sure."

Emotions tangled emotions like a knotted rope yanked hard, because he had her on the phone, he was listening to the sound of her lovely voice and yet she felt so far away. He closed his eyes, shutting out the officers' hootch and the clatter of the heater working hard in the mountain cold. He fought to bring a picture of her into his mind.

What he saw was her that first day in the bookstore, when she'd been awash in the bright, cheerful light of summer. Her hair had glinted like pure gold and fallen in a soft swoop around her lovely face. Her rosy complexion looked as satin-soft as a rose's petal.

His throat ached as he remembered how dainty and sweet she'd looked in a pale-pink sleeveless blouse. But what he wanted was to see her now. To picture her in the solemn shadows of a November's night, when darkness came early in Montana. He could not picture her. Frustration ate at him.

Kelly's voice interrupted the static on the line. "Lexie said it best. She said that your e-mail put her life in perspective, and I felt the same way. The lists I sent, about all the little unimportant things in my day, probably didn't help you much. It probably seemed trite and disrespectful—"

"No, you couldn't be more wrong." No Kevlar vest could protect him from pain like this. Just the thought of her not writing could nearly do him in. "You have no idea how much I appreciate your lists. So, what's this about your mom?"

"Like I said, you didn't call to hear about my mother."

"I called to hear about you."

There he went, trying to get beneath the appearance of things and into a deeper part of her life where she didn't want him to go. "My mom is out of my life. End of story. Some people say that's harsh, that she deserves a second chance, but the truth is that she's on her six-billionth chance, and I just can't take any more. How is your mom doing?"

"Nice change of subject." He didn't sound upset by it, he sounded amused. "Funny you should mention her. I got a pretty interesting e-mail from her. She wanted to know how long I've been seeing you."

"No, that's not true. She couldn't possibly have thought that. I found her number in the phone book a while back—"

"And why would you do that?"

"Well, it's a surprise. Let's just say I wanted to send you something. As one friend to another, of course."

"Sure." He chuckled, as if he understood perfectly. "I bet Mom didn't see it that way. It's just wishful thinking on her part. It's not me she cares about, she said she wanted a daughter-in-law to spoil. She's never forgiven me for being a difficult kid."

"I know that isn't true. When I told her who I was and that I knew you, she went on and on about what a great man she thinks you are."

"Oh, no," he groaned. "She didn't. Really? Now I have to disown her. I can't have a mom embarrassing me like that."

She heard straight through his facade to his big heart beneath. He came from a family like this one, she thought, as she looked around the loving home Amy had made here with her husband and kids. Happiness settled in the air like stardust through the windows. A hundred pictures hung on the wall or were mounted in fat photo albums or were overstuffed in a drawer, waiting for framing. Homemade cookies were fresh in a cookie jar on the table, and love and caring seemed to gleam like moonlight on the polished wood.

Did Mitch know how lucky he was? She thought he did. She hoped he did. "I talked to your mom for less than five minutes, but she seemed like a really lovely lady."

"That would be Mom."

Yes, she thought, he knew. She could hear it in his words. "I'm guessing that when you were growing up, she baked your favorite cookies before you had the chance to ask for them. It sounds like she is still your biggest fan."

"Yeah, everyone needs that in their life. I am blessed with my parents, I know I am. I take it that your mom wasn't the kind of mother who ever baked cookies."

"No." The wounds within her began to reopen, whispers of memories that she *had* to silence.

"Or ever baked a birthday cake?"

"Good guess." She steeled her defenses. She could not let him in any deeper. "My birthday is coming up, and between that and the holidays, she often tries to contact me."

"How much longer does she have on her sentence?"

"I honestly don't know. I expect she'll be out by the end of the year." That's all she wanted to say to him. One more word and she would have opened up too far. "Speaking of time, you should be about halfway through your tour, right?"

"Will she look you up?"

"I hope she doesn't." She squeezed her eyes shut, but that didn't diminish the ugly voices of her past, murmuring in her mother's voice. How she wasn't good enough. Like mother, like daughter. How did she silence those memories? "The last time she got out of prison, she showed up pretending to have missed me, but she stole money out of my backpack when I went to make her some coffee. I'd just gotten paid and that cash was my grocery money for two weeks. I didn't have anything to fall back on."

"I'm sorry, Kelly. You've come a long way on your own."

"I'm not alone."

She touched him deeply, Mitch realized, beyond his comfort level and deeper still, where he'd never felt anything like this before. A fierce steely need to protect her anchored him, and he hated the miles that separated them. "When *is* your birthday?"

"In December."

"What day in December?"

"The second."

Okay, he knew what to do. As he checked his watch, time was ticking away, and he was looking at a hard afternoon of training ahead. But he couldn't hang up yet. He couldn't say good-bye. There was so much he wanted to say, but he was afraid of scaring her off. Afraid of moving too fast. He still didn't know where she stood, if she was moving away from him, or if he could pull her closer.

"Oh, I think I hear the baby." Her heart was showing again. "Let me just whisper, because I don't want to disturb her if she'll fall back to sleep."

He could picture her walking with care down a hallway, to check on a sleeping baby. "Who are you babysitting for tonight?"

"One of the McKaslin cousins, Amy. I've been babysitting for her since Westin, her oldest boy, was three." She paused. "Oh, it looks like little Shannon just needs some comfort. Hello, sweetie. Want me to rub your back? Oh, she's going back to sleep. I was dating Joe then."

"After all this time, they must be like family."

"Family of the heart, that's for sure. Is that what your team members are to you?"

There it was, the depth of her heart in her voice. He felt the distance and the miles melt away. It was a little like being lost in the dark, and she was a beacon lighting the way.

"Like brothers," he confessed. "We spend most of our time together. Sadly, I've got to go before they start without me. But before I do, what are you doing for Thanksgiving?"

"Oh, you're worried that I'll be alone, aren't you? Well, I've turned down Lexie's offer, and Katherine and Spence's offer and Amy's offer to join them for the holiday. I'm going to volunteer again at the free dinner that the local church charities host, and then I'm taking a meal out to my aunt at the hospital."

"I was going to have my mom invite you, if you weren't doing anything."

"That's really nice. But I'm fine. Thanks. What are you doing?"

"I'll be lucky to be here. There's a rumor we're actually getting real turkeys, but I'll have to see it to believe it. I have to go."

Kelly couldn't believe how hard it was to say good-bye. "You'll call again?"

"Count on it." There was a click and he was gone.

Oh, that man could make her feel—make her come alive—like nobody ever had. And wasn't that the problem?

It was as if he was able to see her bare to the soul, where there were no longer any shields, anything safe to hide behind. That left only the truth—of who she'd been and who she was now—and how much she longed to love again.

Longed to love him.

In the quiet of the living room she slipped her phone back into her pack. And thought of Mitch, so far away. Her heart tugged, impossibly, with emotion she could not let in. *Please, Father, watch over him, keep him safe.*

The rain battered the black windows with renewed fury and the ghosts of the past, of the truths she'd spoken of tonight, seemed to whirl in the air around her. The heavens opened as rain hailed against the roof, pounding like a thousand bullets.

She hurried down the hall to check again on the baby, but Shannon was still lost in sweet dreams, safe and soundly asleep. Looking like the precious gift she was.

What a dream it would be to have one of her own, and a life like this. Kelly couldn't help hoping, just a little, and it made the loneliness ache. Careful not to disturb the little one, she tiptoed out of the room and wandered back to her school books, which were waiting for her.

Okay, time to buckle down and concentrate on the attainable dreams in her life. She settled down to study, but every neuron in her head seemed focused on Mitch. On the big, mighty, wonderful, kind man he was.

If she closed her eyes and made a wish, it would look just like him. And wasn't that the danger? Dreams weren't meant for her. She knew that for absolute certain. But it was there, anyway. She'd fought so hard not to let a single hope take root, and it had—for a moment—but she'd dared to let in the smallest wish.

And wasn't that the problem? You started small, with the purest, tiniest wish—and before you knew it, that wish bloomed into a full-fledged, all-of-your-heart dream.

I so want him to love me.

There came the wish, the smallest hope, alive inside her. She screwed her eyes shut against the hot blinding tears that rose. The memory of the day at the river, when Mitch had pulled her against him, protecting her from the current…she wished she had laid her cheek against his chest so she would have known how it felt to be held like that by him. She longed for his tenderness as the stars longed for the night.

And it was impossible. She was in someone else's living room, with the cold November night pressing in around her and she was alone.

Always, endlessly, alone with a dream that could not possibly come true.

Chapter Thirteen

Dear Mitch,

I haven't heard from you since last week when you called. I'm keeping you and your friend Luke in my prayers. And sending warm thoughts your way. The first snow of the season fell today—late for Bozeman—but no one is complaining. Here's a list of good things in my day.

One-dollar movie night at the Garland. We watched *Pride and Prejudice* and ate a vat of fake buttered popcorn. (Lexie says hi.)

Sadly, that was the only good thing in my day. Sending my very best wishes, Kelly

My Dear Kelly,

What do you mean you only had one good thing in your day? Maybe you should add the bad things, too, because I'm not getting an accurate picture here.

Good things in my day: Word is that Luke is gonna pull through. I'm back from stealthing around, but we're going right out on another mission. We had recognizable chow today—at least, we *think* it was chicken.

Sending my prayers, Mitch

Dear Mitch,

I'm so glad for your friend.

The best thing about today was that I recognized everything I ate.

The worst thing about today was that a call came in from the county jail, which Lexie rejected (I wasn't home at the time).

Wherever you are, I hope you're safe and, if not warm, then not too cold.

Keeping you in prayer, Kelly

Dearest Kelly,

I'm sorry about your mom. If I don't get back in time, Happy Thanksgiving. Eat some pie for me.

Always, Mitch

Over the next week, a certain theme had started to emerge in her morning devotional and it was really starting to annoy her. Kelly wished she could take the passage to heart.

I will turn their mourning into gladness; I will
give them comfort and joy instead of sorrow.

This was not helping her stay realistic with her ex-
pectations in life.

In the morning quiet of her apartment, she rubbed
the pad of her forefinger over the text in her devotional. That is *so* not my life, she thought.

She had to prepare herself for the inevitable,
Mitch moving away. And maybe this was it? She'd
had no word from him, nothing. The logical side of
her brain said that he was busy, that was the nature
of his work, to be away from his base camp for days,
or for more than a week at a time.

But the totally non-rational side of her knew that
good-byes were inevitable. She was not going to
give in to the temptation to believe otherwise. With
a thump, she closed the devotional and set it aside.
She concentrated on her second cup of coffee on this
leisurely holiday morning.

She had the apartment to herself. Lexie had
driven home to have Thanksgiving with her parents,
and the bookstore was closed today, of course. It
was a rare thing to have nothing to do and nowhere
to go for an entire morning. She intended to enjoy
it while she could.

The trouble was that loneliness seemed to creep
into the corners of the apartment like the cold air
from outside. Why did her mind automatically

switch to thoughts of Mitch? Of the warm, cozy rumble of his baritone, of the comforting brush of his heart against hers when she talked about her past, and of the way his chuckle, so kind and good-natured, chased away the shadows.

She was letting a wish for Mitch's love and a happy life with him take root in her soul. That was wrong, wrong, wrong. The realization sent fear zinging through her veins. What was she going to do about that? It was simple. Don't think about him. Don't go there. That was the only solution.

She took another sip of her coffee. Where did her thoughts go? To the devotional open on the table in front of her—no, of course not. Her thoughts were thousands of miles away with Mitch, wondering if he'd gotten the rumored turkey for his Thanksgiving Day dinner.

You absolutely have to stop thinking about him, Kelly. She sighed, frustrated at herself. This man was already too far into her heart for safety's sake.

Maybe she'd just get online and send him a happy holidays wish. Then she'd be able to get her mind off him, right? It was worth a try.

While her laptop dialed in, she poured another cup of coffee. But the memory of their last talk remained. How close he'd felt, how carefully he'd listened, how he'd somehow made the past less painful, the shadows less dark. That made no sense whatsoever.

An electronic beep from her laptop interrupted her

thoughts. She brought her cup with her to the table, attention on the screen, her pulse skipping, because what if that was Mitch?

There, on the instant message screen, was an electronic note from Mitchell Dalton.

Kelly
    Happy Thanksgiving. And thanks. That was some care package you sent.
Mitch

Happiness filled her up and buoyed her spirit. She dropped into her chair, already typing.

Mitch
    You got it? Great. I thought it might have been sent to Mars by mistake.
Kelly

Kelly
    I think I saw Mars stamped on the package. I had to beat off the rest of the guys. Apparently candy corns are a great hit with Force Recon marines. Second only to the candy made in the shape of garbage cans.
Mitch

Mitch
    I personally love the bottle-cap ones. Lexie went with me, and we hit every candy counter around

the university. I hope you don't get too sugar-buzzed. Katherine contributed the candy canes and the tin of chocolate sugar crunch cookies.
Kelly

Kelly
   Thank her for me, would you? I'm vibrating from eating all the candy corns. Apparently I didn't learn my lesson when I was six. Hey, are you gonna be home for a while?
Mitch

Mitch
   I'm here for a few more hours. I'm not needed at the church's kitchen until ten-thirty.
Kelly

Kelly
   Then log off and I'll give you a buzz. Deal?
Mitch

   Deal. She hit Send and signed off. She was way too happy that he was calling her. But did she try to hold back her heart? No. She didn't have time to try, because the phone rang and she snatched it up before it could ring twice. "Mitch?"

   "It's me." Yep, he was hooked, Mitch thought, the instant he heard her voice. He felt every inch of the distance that separated them as he leaned back in the metal chair. "Why the church kitchen? Most folks just want to take it easy, not have to work on Thanks-giving."

"I started the year Joe died, when there was an an-nouncement in the church newsletter asking for vol-unteers. It sounded better than spending the day with Joe's family or alone with wishes of what could have been. I liked it, actually, so I've done it ever since."

He wasn't surprised. Classic Kelly, he thought, kindness and sincerity and the greater good. That was just another reason why he was falling in love with her. "Your mom hasn't called again?"

"No, thank goodness. I expect she'll try." Her voice went thin. "I try not to think of her, except when I have to. Did you get a nice dinner?"

"We had meat that was supposed to be the rumored turkey. When we slathered it with the pasty gravy, who could tell? It might have been turkey. I'm happy enough with that. You're a long way away. Tell me what you've been up to. What haven't you put in your e-mails?"

"Like with school?"

"Yeah, school, work, social life."

"What social life? Finals are coming up, so I have a close personal relationship with my textbooks. I'm seeing them exclusively."

"Ah. Still not dating, huh?"

She sounded choked. "You like to get right to the point, don't you? I've given up on dating forever."

"There's some poor man somewhere who is probably pretty broken up to hear that."

"I don't think so. In fact, I'm pretty sure there isn't. There can't be."

A spear of sorrow arrowed through him, it was her pain, he realized, and his pain for her. "Why not?"

"It's not meant to be. You said your friend Luke was doing better?"

"Yeah." He understood why she'd changed the subject. He'd gotten too close. He'd noticed that pattern before. She wanted to keep him at a friendly distance, where she felt safe.

Well, fine, but he was going to push that, if not now, then later, because she would always be safe with him.

But he was coming home in about three weeks' time. He had to know where she stood. The last thing he wanted between them was regret.

"Luke's still recovering. He got hurt pretty bad. Are you thinkin' that I might be next?"

"It crossed my mind."

"Don't let it worry you. I won't be. Besides, just living is risky business."

"Yeah, but we're friends. That gives me the prerogative to worry about you."

"Then I'll worry about you and we'll be even."

"What risky things do I do? Oh, I know. You're going to say that I drive."

"Yep, you get in a car every day. That's risky stuff, too." He hated the distance between them, the miles that kept him from reaching out to her and pulling her into his arms and holding her until she believed.

Until she could see he had no plans to break her heart. "Is that why you aren't dating? You're afraid of caring about someone and losing them again?"

"Something like that." Her voice sounded sturdy, strong.

But he could feel the waver of emotion; he could feel how vulnerable she was. "The package you sent, it meant a lot."

"Good, because I wanted it to. You helped me when I really needed it." Her tone was friendly, but her heart betrayed her.

At least, he wanted to think it was her heart he felt, even half a world away. "Are you talking about the little bit of help I gave you on quadratic equations?"

"It made the difference between an A and a B. I know that doesn't sound like very much, but it does to me. I have a four-point grade average, and I'd like it to stay that way, since I'm looking at graduate school next year."

No, this was more than a thank-you. He looked down at the good-sized cardboard box stuffed with candy. Candy shaped like garbage cans, like pop-bottle tops, fruit and people. There was taffy and bubble gum and jawbreakers in every color, gummy bears and gummy worms and long red ropes of still soft and still mealy licorice.

And not only candy, but animal cookies and cheese snacks and gum and the latest military suspense he'd been wanting, cupcakes and Twinkies and packages of beef jerky. At the bottom of the box was an MSU T-shirt, extra-large. She'd sent books of word jumbles and crossword puzzles and a travel-sized chess set.

Not an ordinary care package. He knew, because his mom sent them all the time. Shoeboxes stuffed with homemade brownies, not boxes full of all kinds of stuff that took time and thought to put together. Kelly might say they were friends, but her actions and the emotion in her words said more.

Good to know, since he was walking without cover. Heaven knew he was feeling out of his depth. He was a Force Recon marine, he knew how to be patient, when to wait and when to take a step forward. "You want to go to graduate school there in Bozeman, or are you looking to go somewhere else?"

"I'd like to stay here. I have to be accepted to the program first."

"You will. I believe in you, Kelly."

What on earth could she say to that? Kelly squeezed her eyes shut. Did he have to say those words as if with all the tenderness in his big heart? He made her feel like a new, twinkling star; he also stirred up pain. Like a powerful river's current, scudding along the bottom of the river bed, scraping up raw places and exposing them, the places within her that longed to love again.

But Mitch was right. It hurt too much to let

someone in—especially him. What she had to do was stop this, before she'd taken another step on a path leading to where she didn't want to go. How could she let him into her heart any farther? It already hurt too much.

"Mitch, I don't think—" She bit her lips, torn apart by pain. By fear. "I value our *friendship,* but—" That's all I can do, she thought.

"I value you pretty highly, too."

The certainty in his voice frightened her as much as the tenderness in his words. It was a tenderness she could feel as if his emotions were coming right through the long-distance line, too, and into her heart.

I could love him so much. *If* things were different. If I were different.

How did she tell him that?

There was a rustle, as if he'd dropped the phone, and in the background it sounded like men were shouting. "I gotta go." It was all he said before he hung up, leaving her with an empty line.

What had happened? Was he okay? She tried to banish all the images of war she'd seen on televised news reports and told herself maybe it was a high wind, knocking out the phone connection. It didn't mean something horrible had happened.

She tasted fear as she hung up the phone. Her fingers trembled as she pulled the cup of lukewarm coffee into her hands. Fear for him double-beat through her veins and into her soul.

Please, keep him safe, Lord. It was the only thing she could do for him, so she prayed.

She could not stop the sick cold dread that had followed her all through her day and crept into her like the night's chill. Shivering from the bitter winds and covered with snow, Kelly gratefully turned the deadbolt on her apartment door behind her. The roads had been terribly icy, but she'd made it home safely in one piece.

Her day had been a busy one, but Mitch had stayed in the forefront of her thoughts, where he was still as she shrugged off her coat and hung it over the back of a chair to dry.

She pulled her cell from the pocket. No calls. She knew it hadn't rung, but she had to check anyway. It was another sign that she already cared dangerously too much for this man.

As she turned up the thermostat, she noticed the time. Eight fifty-three. No way was she going to be able to wind down enough to sleep anytime soon. Her mind was spinning with all the horrible possibilities she wouldn't quite let herself imagine—and her stomach was one nauseated knot, as it had been all day.

I'm afraid for him. She couldn't deny it. She'd sent so many prayers skyward, surely every angel in heaven had heard them by now. She dropped her stuff on the floor and sank onto the edge of the couch. What was she going to do? She ached with regret. With all the ways she would never be able to care for this man.

With all the ways she wanted to.

In the silence of the night-dark apartment she fought to keep the past from coming alive. From seeing Joe's coffin, polished black in the funeral home, feeling the shattered pieces of her heart like broken glass shards, impossible to put back together. Her mother's words resonated in her head. "I told you. Didn't I tell you?"

She choked down the rest, forcing the images and sounds and feelings back down behind lock and key. If only she could wipe them away like an eraser over a chalkboard. Life wasn't like that.

To help chase away the shadows and the silence, she clicked on the TV and surfed, looking for something that caught her attention. But what she really wanted was for the phone to ring and Mitch's voice to be on the other end of the line.

She paused over the cable news channels for anything that would possibly concern him, but there was nothing there, and she really didn't expect there to be. He's fine, he's said over and over how well-trained he is. And, she thought, he certainly is a capable man, but that didn't break apart the concern that sat like an iceberg in the middle of her chest.

She didn't need one more sign. Look at how much she was hurting for him. Over him. This is too much, she told herself and buried her face in her hands. She wanted him to be safe with all of her might, but one thing was clear.

She was overinvolved. She cared too much. She *had* to stop ignoring the truth.

I'm in love with him. She was starting to dream, to let hope for a happy life with Mitch begin to grow. And wasn't that the worst mistake ever?

The snowstorm raged and thunder cannoned overhead. She sat unmoving while the darkness at the edge of the lamplight's reach deepened like despair. The phone rang once. Twice.

She leaned far enough over the arm of the couch to read the caller ID on the living-room extension. Out of area. The same area code Mitch had called from earlier in the day.

Good, he was safe, thank God, that's all she needed to know.

She let it ring.

Chapter Fourteen

It's probably the intensive study week right before finals—that's why Kelly hadn't e-mailed him. Mitch rubbed his hands together in the cold hootch. The heaters had conked out again—they couldn't keep up with the cold. Maybe he'd send another e-mail, just so he would feel as if he'd done something instead of letting her slip away.

He started typing.

My Dear Kelly,

Sorry again that I had to cut our talk short. I know you're busy getting ready for finals, but here's another list. It's the good things I wish for you.

Easy finals that you breeze right through. Ice-free roads wherever you travel. Eggnog lattes steaming hot, every time you need one. I hope you get plenty of time to relax, take time for friends and that you have no regrets.

I'll be out, but I'll keep you in my prayers.
Love and fellowship, Mitch

And, he thought, he'd keep her in his heart. It wasn't
enough, he thought as he sent the letter whizzing
through cyberspace, but it was *all* he could do.

He'd leave the rest in God's hands.

"Did that poor man call *again?*" There was no mistaking the disapproval in Lexie's voice as she drizzled
melted butter over the two heaping bowls of popcorn.
"I say the gender is entirely untrustworthy, but there's
always an exception to every rule, and I think Mitch
is that rare exception. You should date him."

"No way. Especially not him." She didn't mention
that she had his latest e-mail on her screen. That
she'd gotten online to do some research at the library
and what did she do? Check her e-mail just to see his
name listed in her inbox.

What did that say? That she'd fallen hard for him.
And that was one truth she could hardly admit to, and
it was a truth she had to change.

She studied the half dozen e-mails he'd sent, one
for every day that had passed since they'd spoken.
The first apologizing for hanging up on her, that
there had been some kind of attempt to attack their
base camp, the second came posted near midnight
his time, that they'd successfully tracked down the
insurgents, and everyone in camp was safe. And of

the remaining four e-mails, each was more concerned than the last. He was reaching out to her.

How did she tell him to stop reaching? To stop pushing? He wanted friendship. And she wanted…well, it was better not to put *that* into words.

"Why especially him?" Lexie wanted to know as she reached for the salt shaker.

"Because that man is a dream."

"Yeah. Duh. He ought to be your dream and you're going to lose this chance with him."

"A chance at what? He's stationed in California. He's just a friend. Here, let me read this." She pointed at the screen for emphasis. "'That you take time for friends.' He wrote that because I'm not e-mailing him back. He thinks I'm busy. So, we're friends. See? Just friends."

Lexie slipped one of the bowls on the table next to the laptop. She studied the screen doubtfully. "I saw the way he looked at you, and it has *nothing* to do with friendship."

"Exactly what does that mean?"

"Hey, don't get angry at the messenger." Lexie scooped the other bowl from the counter and filled her hand with the fluffy popped corn. "Mitch looks at you like you're a morning star he'd plucked from the sky to dream on. Write him or call him. I mean it, Kelly. He's one of the good guys."

Wasn't that the problem? And why was she so mad at him all of a sudden? Mad that he was so wonderful and perfect, that if he had been anything less than that, she wouldn't be hurting like this. She wouldn't be torn between the past and the present, between the lonely road she'd chosen and everything she was afraid of.

He wasn't hers to keep, but there was love in her heart for him anyway.

"Well, think about it." Lexie settled down on the couch and turned her attention to her schoolbooks.

I don't have to think about it. She knew exactly what had to be done. She hadn't realized how far he'd crept into her heart, but fearing for him showed her exactly how much she cared. She couldn't go back and pretend the interrupted phone call hadn't happened. She couldn't deny how deeply she'd been afraid for him or the breadth of her caring.

But neither could she take one more step on this path. She was in love with him. She didn't *want* to be in love with him because it was going to lead to heartache.

Be sensible, Kelly. She steeled her heart and gathered her defenses. She clicked closed the e-mail screen and typed in the library's address. She had priorities. She had her own goals, goals that would still be within her reach when Mitch was back safely from his tour and in California, where he belonged.

And if that broke her heart, it was only the truth. She'd learned the hard way never to dream.

* * *

Being really cold wasn't half-bad, once you got used to it. Mitch gulped down the dregs at the bottom of his C-4 cup of coffee and considered his current problem. He hunkered into his sleeping bag and considered his options.

He had second watch, so there was no sense to going to sleep for an hour, and with so much on his mind and the subzero temps in the small cavelet they'd found for the night, it would take him that long just to shiver himself warm enough to fall asleep.

His real problem was what to do about Kelly. He knew he wouldn't find an e-mail waiting for him when he got back to camp. Had he scared her off with his talk of dating and the future? Well, he'd just wanted to know where he stood and how he could make this work. Surely the good Lord hadn't brought him this far only for heartache.

Next to him Pierce was snoring, sound asleep. The next bag over Mark was writing to his wife. That's what he was thinking of doing too, except he was pretty sure Kelly hadn't written him back. She was moving away from him. He could feel it in his heart, like a light dimming.

Right now, there was nothing he could do about it. Not one thing. He only knew that he wouldn't be able to call her on her birthday like he'd wanted. It would be days before he had the chance to call, and who knew what mission after that? He was losing her.

Or was it already too late?

Lord, I need help on this one. Please. There came no answer in the frigid night.

In the pleasant warmth of the bookstore, with Christmas decorations cheering up the floor and customers shopping to the sound of holiday carols in the background, Kelly *should* have had enough on her mind with ringing up sales, gift-wrapping and helping shoppers.

In theory, she shouldn't have a free brain cell to spare, but she obviously did. And what was she doing with it? Going over her notes in her memory because her first final was cumulative and would be here before she knew it? No, she was thinking of Mitch's last e-mail. The one she'd sworn not to read, and then gone right ahead and read it.

Apparently she needed to ask for more willpower in her prayers tonight.

Kindly Mrs. Finch, her very favorite customer, ambled up to the cash wrap and slid a beautifully illustrated Bible on the counter. "Thank you so very much, young lady, for this wonderful suggestion. It's perfect. My great-granddaughter will treasure it."

"I'm sure she'll treasure you more, Opal. Would you like me to gift-wrap this for you?"

"That would be wonderful, dear. I would like the paper with the golden angels."

"It will look really nice, I promise. And there's a coupon on this, so I'll ring it up at the lower price."

"That's good of you. I surely do appreciate the savings."

Kelly grabbed an in-house charge form and a pen. "This will just take a moment to wrap. You could get a cup of hot apple cider and wait in the reading area. That way you can put your feet up and relax."

"I'll do that, then." Opal's smile was as pure as always. "You and I haven't taken time to catch up. You must be working hard at your college studies."

"You know I am." Kelly rang up the sale and presented Opal with her copy of the charge slip. "Finals are coming up. You and I need to compare notes about the devotional."

"Oh, my!" Opal lit up as she slipped the charge slip into her cavernous purse. "It uplifts my spirits every day. Did you get a chance to read today's yet? 'My purpose is that they may be encouraged in heart and united in love.'"

"I did." Kelly was doing her very best not to dwell on it as she found a gift box on one of the lower shelves beneath the register. Time to change the subject. "Your great-granddaughter is hoping to get into MSU, right?"

"Now, don't change the subject, dear. I want to hear all about that handsome soldier who was so sweet on you." Opal looked delighted. "Spence mentioned him the last time I was in. Is he still serving overseas?"

"Yes, he is, and he's not sweet on me. Spence needs a talking-to." There was no venom behind her words; how could she fault Joe's cousin who was always looking out for her? He meant well. He simply didn't understand. "Mitch is only a friend."

"I'm sorry to hear that. He was such a strapping young man." Opal smiled knowingly as she turned away, adding over her shoulder, "Remember, there's more to life than studying. But don't take my advice. Turn to Scripture, dear."

This morning's devotional text popped into her mind. "My purpose is that they may be encouraged in heart and united in love."

Why did that feel so much like *not* a coincidence? Maybe because it couldn't be a sign. She refused to mistake it for one. No matter what. She would not be fooled again.

As she placed a torn-off sheet of the fragile golden-foil angel wrapping paper on the counter, the bell above the door announced another customer. Kelly recognized Holly from the jewelry shop a few blocks down, a close friend of Katherine's. "Hi, Holly, Katherine's in her office. Go right in."

"Actually, I'm here to see you." Holly set the small tasteful gift bag she was carrying on the counter. "This is from Mitch. Happy birthday."

"What?" Kelly stared at the bag, small and dainty.

Only one thing could fit in a bag that small—the lovely jewelry that Holly made. "From Mitch?"

"He contacted me from his base. He'd had me hold this for him ever since you two were in my shop last summer." Holly slipped around the corner. "He must really be fond of you."

Mitch. She could only stare, stunned, at his thoughtfulness. He'd remembered her birthday. He'd remembered—no, he'd known at the time how much she'd admired the beautiful jewelry. Surely he hadn't bought the pearl angel she'd liked. No, he hadn't done that. He couldn't have. Because then that would mean *way too much*.

"Open it," Katherine said from her doorway, with a secret smile that said she'd known about this for some time. She disappeared into her office with Holly, but they left the door ajar.

Kelly's hands were shaking. A customer was approaching, shopping basket brimming, and she set the bag on the back counter. She resisted the temptation to glance inside because it would only make the locks around her heart buckle a tiny bit more.

"I'll get this." Spence stepped in with his no-nonsense attitude and stern manner, but there was a hint of a smile at the corners of his mouth as he took over her till. "You go take a break."

"Not until I get Mrs. Finch's Bible gift-wrapped." She stubbornly turned to her work, the gift bag glinting with foil threads of silver and gold.

Mitch. How was she going to keep hold of her senses now? His thoughtfulness touched her in the worst possible places. Her love for him remained, dazzling and enduring even as she fought it.

"Open the gift," Spence told her between ringing up sales. "It's your birthday. It shouldn't be a day of all work and no celebration."

"But that's why I'm here." She folded the last corner on Mrs. Finch's gift and taped it down neatly. "I'll open it later, when we're not so busy."

"What am I going to do with you?" Stern, Spence shook his head and frowned at her, but the concern in his eyes betrayed him.

She didn't know what she was going to do with herself either. She could not let herself start believing in fairy tales and happily ever afters. She was not Cinderella. She would not take a single step off her chosen path, the safe one God had graciously given her to walk. See what heartache came from dreaming? From wishing, just a little?

She secured a generous length of ribbon and made an extravagant bow on Mrs. Finch's package, slipped it into a shopping bag with a few coupons and complimentary sugar-free candy canes, and delivered it to Opal, who was enjoying a cup of apple cider and was pleased with the wrapping.

The store was busy with holiday shoppers, moms toting their babies or pushing strollers, families bursting with secrets as they browsed the store. It was like looking at the pieces of her broken hopes, seeing the happiness around her. The first year losing Joe had broken her to the core, and she had finally, two years after that, come to a numb acceptance.

Deep in her heart, in the secret quiet places only God knew, was the little girl's wish for a real family, a place to belong and someone to cherish with all of her heart. She used to believe God's promise that there would be good in her life. And love, which was the greatest of all.

But here she was, twenty-five today, with plenty of blessings and a calling to do good in this world, and what was she doing? Wishing for more than she deserved. And she knew it. Why? Because at the back of her mind she was waiting for the other shoe to fall. It was her birthday. That could only mean one thing.

"I want to see this gift," Katherine told her, after seeing Holly to the door. "Go into my office if you want some privacy first, but Kelly, this is a big deal."

"No, it's a birthday gift, something thoughtful, but it doesn't mean—"

"It does. You're still in contact with him, right?"

Kelly felt the twist of pain but she swallowed it down. Mitch. Each passing day she'd thought of him. Each day she'd resisted checking her e-mail. How did she explain? She didn't understand it herself. "I'm not dating him. You know that we're just friends."

"That's how it starts, you know."

"How what starts?"

"The real thing. True love. Happily ever after. It starts with being best friends. At least, that's what they tell me. I know, I know, you're going to start arguing with me, and that's okay. As long as you remember that as much as we all wished you could have married Joe and you'll always be a member of our family at heart, you need to move on. Find the blessings God has in store for you."

"Oh, Katherine, please don't break my heart like that." There was the past, the dreaded past, rising up like a tidal wave threatening to pull her into an ocean of feelings she did not want to face. She swallowed past the hopelessness. "Believe me, I have so much in my life to be thankful for. I have enough."

"I know the hard way—it's not enough. Life isn't quite as sweet or as meaningful without someone to love deeply."

Kelly couldn't speak past the emotions in her throat. In her heart. Weighing down her soul. She was hardly aware of Katherine steering her, along with Mitch's gift, into the cozy comfort of the corner office.

What did she do? If she didn't look inside the gift bag, then she wouldn't have to face the truth she'd been afraid of all along. She loved Mitch. He might feel more than friendship for her. Nothing could terrify her more.

Her chest clogged tight, as if buried under the

weight of her broken dreams. She couldn't take one more loss. One more good-bye. I will not step off this path.

She swiped hot tears from her eyes, feeling as if her spirit was ripping down to the quick. It was fear that filled the cracked places and the wounded places inside her. Terror of being hurt like that again because she'd believed in the impossible.

I cannot believe in this. In what she could never have. Her finger shook as she pulled the small box from the bag. She already knew what she would find as she cradled the jeweler's box in the palm of her hand, but her pulse stalled at the gleam of pearl, and the shimmer of delicate gold that made up the halo and wings of an angel.

A small gift card said, "Here's a guardian angel to watch over you until I get back and can do the job."

Mitch. Did he have any idea what he was doing to her? She was breaking apart, the safeguards she'd built around herself crumbling like clay, exposing the raw, most vulnerable places that longed to believe. The heart of the girl she used to be when she believed in fairy tales and in dreams coming true.

When she'd believed God would find a way one day to give her real love and a place to belong.

Maybe this is your chance. The hope came in the quiet between heartbeats. It came from the deepest parts of her soul. Hope burned like banked embers breathing back to life.

I so want to love this man. What was she going to do? And even if he loved her in return…

No, don't go there. She closed the door on that thought and locked it away. No more wishes. Not one single hope. She replaced the lid on the box, and slipped the box into the gift bag.

If only she could put away the feelings in her heart as easily.

Lord, help take this wish from my heart. Please.

There was no answer. Only the constant slanting fall of the snowflakes outside the window and the faint musical rendition of "Silent Night" from the store's stereo system.

She'd never felt more alone.

Chapter Fifteen

The parking-lot lights beamed a safe path from the pizza parlor all the way to their parked cars. Since her arms were full with the pizza box of leftovers and bags of gifts from her party, Kelly held the door with her shoulder for her friends.

Lexie caught the door handle and helped her, juggling the remains of a cake. "What do you say we hit the ice creamery? We could car-pool over. The roads look icy. I've got four-wheel drive."

"Sounds good to me." Jessica commented as she filed outside, zipping her parka snug. "I don't have to hurry home. How about you, Rose?"

"Count me in." Rose brought up the rear, pulling on her mittens.

It had been fairly easy not to have to think about Mitch's gift, which was tucked safely in her backpack's front pocket. But now, with the icy snowflakes brushing her cheeks and the momentary quiet as they all negotiated the icy parking lot without falling, Kelly had a split second where Mitch crowded her mind.

Maybe it was because the greasy, pepperoni tang of warm pizza drifted up through the lid of the pizza box she carried, reminding her of the bright summer night he'd shown up with pizza in hand and had affably watched the romantic comedy Lexie had picked up at the video store.

Just the remembered feeling of being in his presence that day made peace trickle all the way down to her soul. That peace remained through the hour spent at the ice cream shop and into the quiet of her bedroom where she studied, huddled in her flannel pajamas and fleece slippers, while the baseboard heater tried to keep up with the cold seeping in through the window and walls.

Why was she hurting like this? Everything within her ached like a snapped bone, and she couldn't concentrate at all on her studies. As pointless as it was, she took Mitch's gift from her backpack and opened the small box. In the bright reading lamp, the delicate angel's lacey wings and lustrous pearl gown gleamed like a promise.

This was no minor trinket and not a simple gift. This had come from his heart. She rubbed her fingers over the black inked words, written in a delicate script, probably Holly's, but she knew they were

Mitch's words. "Here's a guardian angel to watch over you until I get back and can do the job."

Katherine's words from today troubled her. *The real thing. True love. Happily ever after. It starts with being best friends.*

She forced the fears and the whispers from the past aside.

Is there a way, Lord? Could Mitch really be meant for me? Every cell of her being hurt with the wish. In the deepest places within her soul, she wanted to believe. But was it possible?

Losing Joe still had a hold on her. How did she find enough faith to believe that the future could be different? That there were good things waiting for her, good things that wouldn't be jerked from her the minute she reached for them?

The phone rang. When she checked the caller ID, it was out of area, from an area code she didn't recognize. It was her birthday, and that was often a day her mom tried to contact her, but what if it was Mitch calling?

"I bet it's Mitch," Lexie called from her room.

I bet it is, too. It would be just like him to call tonight. She lifted the receiver, longing for the warmth of his baritone and a connection to him, and terrified of it at the same time. "Hello?"

There was no crackle on the line, no overseas static. The hesitation was all wrong. She knew who it was before she heard her mother say her name. "Kelly? Is that really my sweet baby?"

I should have had Lexie answer it, Kelly realized, too late. The voices from her past rose up, and there were no defenses strong enough to stop them. Memories she'd held down for so long crashed like a tidal wave, making the past so immediate and vivid she could taste the hollowness and desolation. She knew this was part of her mom's pattern—she'd try to make up and then the pleas for money would start. Then the stealing.

"Mom," she managed to choke out. "You're not supposed to call me. The court said you can't."

"But you're my own little girl."

How many times had she heard that phrase? When she'd been six years old, holding her mom's hair when she was sick from being drunk. When she was ten years old and her mother was high on drugs. When she was twelve years old and they had lost their apartment and were standing in line at a shelter.

Stop it. She squeezed her eyes shut, gritting her teeth, but the images just kept coming. Her mom's anger when Kelly had wanted to live with her aunt Louise. The calls and every attempt to visit whenever Kelly had her life finally leveling out. Her mom arriving uninvited at Joe's funeral and whispering, after the service, "It's just as well he's gone. You might as well learn it now. No one's gonna love you enough to last, girl. You're too much like me."

For once, Kelly broke the pattern and hung up the phone. It was as if all the footholds she'd built to hold up her life buckled and came crashing down. What if her mother was right? That's exactly how it felt. What if every time her life became stable, all it took was her past to knock it down? What if the foundations of her life, her beginnings in life, were not strong enough to support a good future? Whatever the case, Kelly couldn't allow her mother back in her life until the woman made a significant effort to heal.

As time ticked by she placed the jeweler's box into her backpack. After a while, the dark shadows did not seem so bleak. The memories of the girl she'd been, heart wide open waiting to belong, faded away.

She didn't know how long it was until the phone rang again, and Lexie hurried through the doorway. "We'll just turn off the ringer. Is there anything I can do?"

Kelly shook her head.

"I'll make you some tea. My mom says honey and chamomile tea makes anything a little bit better." Lexie disappeared.

Kelly reached for her Bible. She knew that the Lord worked all things for the good of His faithful. Sometimes it was all she could do to believe, but she held on to her faith with both white-knuckled hands and did not let go.

In the bleak gray of the rugged eastern Afghanistan landscape, Mitch huddled with his team. The spot they'd chosen was well-hidden from the road below, and it offered good protection from the cruel wind whipping down from the glaciered peaks. Hunkered down, they should be undetectable, but he stayed on high alert.

Pierce leaned close, speaking in a voice lower than a whisper. "Not a lot of activity. Doesn't feel right, though."

"Nope. Like we're in the crosshairs." It wasn't a good sign when the hunters felt hunted. He scanned the lower, opposing slope with his gun scope.

Nothing. Maybe it would stay that way. A few more hours, they would radio command, and come dark, extraction. He'd be on a bird out of here.

And then he felt it, as if a steady light in his heart winked out. It was Kelly. She was gone, just like that, and he knew that he'd lost her love. That she had let go of him.

And there was nothing he could do about it.

Hopeless, Kelly opened the window blinds so she could feel the gray light of dawn fall across her face. Exhaustion settled around her like the freezing fog outside, cloaking her, keeping her numb. Her heart beat dully, without feeling, like the deadness that follows a great shock.

Or a great loss.

How can I do this? How can I find the words to tell Mitch good-bye? Rising tears burned in her throat.

Outside the window, freezing fog shrouded the

treetops and veiled the sky and mountains from view. Snow mantled the world, clung to the barren poplar limbs, covered the sidewalks and street and rooftops below, and frosted the view like icing on a cake. The gray cold seeped into her soul.

Being alone was the truth of her life. A truth she'd learned to accept the hard way. She didn't want any more lessons teaching her that. The ones she'd had so far had been painful enough. She couldn't go through that loss one more time.

You have to let him go, Kelly. She felt the past whisper. Felt the pain of Joe's loss rising up through the numbness. The wounds within her began to reopen, whispers of memories that she could no longer silence. Joe, who'd come from the black-sheep branch of the McKaslin family, who'd grown up with his dad in and out of jail, who'd understood. How her greatest fear in life was that her mother was right.

How would Mitch understand?

What if God had already worked a miracle in her life, bringing her on this path instead of into a desperate life like her mother's? What if this was the great good meant for her and there would be nothing more?

Down deep, she knew, if she took one step off this path and risked her heart again, everything would crumble. She'd had that lesson over and over again. Fear clawed through her, sharp-taloned and relentless.

I don't need to hurt like that one more time.

Letting him go was the sensible thing to do. It was

the right thing to do, the safest decision. Just do it, Kelly. Stop procrastinating. Do the right thing.

She stared at her computer screen, alone in the apartment, heartsick. How was she going to say good-bye? She had no heart left to feel with. No faith left over to try to believe. Even if he was her dream come true. Even if he was everything wonderful and noble and good she'd ever believed in. Summer felt so far away, with the bright green world and bold sunshine and the rumble of Mitch's laughter as he'd hauled her out of the cool river.

That's how it starts, Katherine's words came back to her. *The real thing. True love. It starts with being best friends.*

She buried her face in her hand and remained perfectly still, letting the past settle down, hoping the memories would release her, but they didn't. There was no solace, no comfort as the heater clicked on, whirring under the curtains, which swayed and billowed. The pain and emptiness of her past was nothing compared to the anguish of this moment without Mitch. And of all the moments to come without him.

She covered her mouth, stopping the sob from escaping. Nothing could stop the grief shattering her soul.

I'm so sorry, Mitch. She was a realist these days, and not a dreamer. She would keep both feet on the ground. Mitch was not hers to keep. Not now. Not ever.

All the prayers in the world wouldn't change it.

Her vision blurred as she placed her trembling fingertips above the keys. Just when she thought she couldn't take another good-bye, here she was, typing that dreaded word that cut like a blade through her soul.

Battle-weary and heartsick, Mitch wasn't at all surprised to see a single e-mail from Kelly waiting for him. He was exhausted, the images on the screen blurred. He scrubbed his eyes and tried to focus.

This could not be good news. He could feel it in his gut, the same way he'd known in the bush deep in enemy territory that things were about to go south.

Retreat would be safer.

He opened the e-mail and felt as he had on the side of the mountain, as if he were caught in a rifle's scope.

Dear Mitch
First of all, I hope you are safe and well. I care about you and I always will, and I want good things for you and your life.

He rubbed his beard, greasy from face paint, and tried to calm the shock settling in his chest. He'd known this was waiting for him. That wasn't what surprised him. It was that she was really doing it, that there was no way to undo this. He was half a world away and it might as well be the whole universe separating them. She was ending it. No, he corrected, feeling the void in his heart. She already had.

I'll always be glad you walked into the bookstore that bright summer day. You have no idea how much I will treasure this time I've spent being your friend, but I have to say good-bye. Although I was touched by it, I can't accept your gift. Finals start next week, and I'm going to be too busy to e-mail, and by the time they're done, you'll be home in California and you'll have no more need for a pen pal, I'm sure, so I'll just say good-bye. Kelly

Good-bye. He stopped breathing at her words. It took a moment to sink in. She was returning the gift. Pretending all that had ever been between them was a pen-pal thing.

His heart broke, piece by piece, cracking all the way down to his soul. How could she end it like this?

"Dalton." It was Scott, the corpsman, lumbering into the hootch looking as haggard as Mitch felt. "I gotta take a look at your arm."

"It's nothing. Just a little shrapnel."

"After you hit the shower and chow, stop by and let me look at it. You'll need stitches."

"Nah. I'm good." It wasn't the jagged gash or the hunk of metal he'd pulled out of it that was his problem.

"You'd better come, or I'll hunt you down," Scott called over his shoulder on his way out.

The hootch was empty this time of day, and the sounds of other teams training outside faded into the background. Mitch rubbed his forehead with the heel of his hand. How was he going to fix this? Was it possible? It had to be. *Right, Lord?*

No answer. He'd halfway expected one, he thought as he thumbed a calling card from his pocket. How could he have lost so much in a single day? He hauled his overtired body out of the metal chair. It was 0400 in her part of the world. He'd call her after he showered and put some food in his gut. Maybe by then he would have mastered this pain. Maybe by then he would have figured out a way to fix this.

He knew one thing for sure. He would not give up, he would not give in, and he would not go down. Nothing in his life had ever mattered like this. Kelly was his heart's choice.

No matter what.

He prayed to God that he could still be her choice, too.

In the cocoon of the university's library, Kelly chose an empty table next to the stacks. All around her other students were busy studying, reading or re-searching. She had a few more facts to look up for her term paper, which was due tomorrow. As she unzipped her laptop case, she noticed an ROTC student in his uniform seated two tables over.

Mitch. Her life had been just fine until he'd first walked into the bookstore. From that moment, her life had changed. She hadn't realized it, but coming to know him and fall in love with him had filled a place in her soul she hadn't known was empty. A place that had never been filled before.

It was empty now, like her life. How had he come to mean so much to her? Mitch had become a part of her day. She hadn't realized all the time she'd spent thinking about him, or finding fun things to tell him in e-mails, or looking forward to checking her inbox and seeing his name there.

Every time she'd turned on the TV, she'd checked the news channels. When she saw the reports and footage of the devastation left by car bombings, or reports of the latest military conflict far from home, she knew that Mitch was out there with his men and his weapons and his skills doing his best to protect freedom.

And his gift…the image of his words were etched in her mind. He wanted the job of watching over her.

How had it come to this? How had she let it?

Forget his strength and tenderness. Forget the joy he'd brought to her life. Forget the emotional connection he'd made to her heart.

Forgetting wasn't so easy. Longing filled her, an unstoppable love for Mitch. With every breath she took, it was as if more love filled her up. More affection for him. She couldn't stop it. She wasn't strong enough to stop it.

Take this love for him from my heart, Lord. Please.

There was no answer. Just the one in her heart growing stronger and more true. Right along with the dreams she knew better than to let herself start believing.

In the purposeful activity of the staging area, Mitch shivered in the open air, despite the adrenaline kicking through his veins. He was packed and good to go, except for this one last thing. Impatient, he waited for the satellite phone to connect.

So far away, the line began to ring in Kelly's apartment. He counted the rings above the drone of the prepping helicopters. Two. Three. Four.

C'mon, Kelly, pick up. Gritting his teeth, he waited, his heart dark and empty. Four rings. Five.

He bowed his head. *Please let her answer, Lord. I'm out of time here.*

Six rings. Then an electronic beep. He hung on, he needed to talk to her. He needed this fixed before he went out. Then he heard it, her voice. Her sweet soft voice.

"Please leave a message," was all she said. The gentle sound was like a guiding light in a dark storm, and eased some of the pain down deep.

He scrubbed his hand over his face. Leaving a

message was the last thing he wanted. "Kelly, if you're there. Pick up."

Nothing. He knew she was there. Rent down to the soul, he did the only thing left. He told her the truth.

"I'm headed out on a pretty serious mission. I don't know when I'll be back. I just…want to know what I did wrong."

He waited, *feeling* her on the other end, listening to him. He knew what the losses she had suffered could do to a person. He was guilty of some of that himself—closing your heart off and staying distant to keep from getting too close and feeling too much. It was easier.

But it was no way to live. Maybe God had led him to Kelly, because she needed more.

And, Mitch was man enough to admit, he needed more, too.

He cleared the raw emotion from his throat. "You are an awesome blessing in my life, and I—" Love you more than I thought possible, he didn't say, he held back the truth, the frightening truth because he could feel her rejection ready to fall like a thrown grenade.

"Don't forget me." It was all he could say before his throat closed. He loved her. No matter what. And that love, even if she could not return it, remained, not fading, and not budging.

I'll be back, he promised as he handed back the phone, grabbed his MP-5, ready to roll.

Lord, please keep her heart open to me, he prayed. But a cold fear began to gnaw at him. What if there was no way to fix this? What if it was too late?

His future stretched out before him without her, without light. Like the sun going down on his life.

Safe in the warmth of her apartment, Kelly turned away from the answering machine, pressed her face in her hands and fought the bleak, heartbreaking grief. The last hope within her had died.

Letting him go wasn't easy. It *was* the best thing. The safest decision for them both.

But it didn't feel that way. Neither determination, nor distance, nor her own fears could halt the love she felt for him. She feared nothing could.

At least it was over, she thought with relief. She had her path in life, and Mitch had his.

Chapter Sixteen

It was Christmas Eve, and Kelly was thankful she had volunteered to work at the bookstore until closing. It kept her from thinking, and since her thoughts always wandered to Mitch, it was a good thing to keep busy. It was easier to ignore her shattered heart that way.

As she carefully removed the porcelain figurine from the front window display she had a perfect view of the dark parking lot as an SUV pulled off the street and maneuvered through the snow.

Although the snowfall obscured all but the headlights from her sight, the vehicle parked right in front, beneath the filtered glow of the tall security lights. The driver's door open and a booted foot hit the ground. Her pulse jerked to a stop.

That was a military boot, just like Mitch wore. No, it can't be him. She froze, the warmth of the store, the caroling of the sound systems, the frantic bustle of last-minute shoppers faded into nothing.

There was only the sight of the soldier dressed in camouflage climbing from his vehicle. One look at his wide shoulders and joy speared through her soul.

Mitch. The cry came from the deepest part of her being. In the exact same split second her eyes registered that the man wasn't as tall or as powerfully muscled, and, as he cut through the light crossing in front of the vehicle, he wasn't Mitch.

Disappointment left her arctic cold. The pain of it left her light-headed, but she could not look away from the soldier, who opened the passenger door and helped a woman from the front seat.

Kelly could only stare, captivated, by the sight of the soldier and his wife as they gazed into one another's eyes for a brief moment—a moment that seemed to stretch timelessly—before he turned to lift a baby in a carrier from the back seat. The loving family was straight out of her most secret dreams.

It was like looking at what might have been, what could have been.

What still might be, her heart whispered so strongly.

It can never be, she thought firmly. Hadn't she put all her foolish wishes to rest?

The couple approached the front door, and the soldier released his wife's hand to open it for her. They smiled loving, quiet smiles to one another, clearly bonded in love.

Broken pieces of her dreams were all around her, but she managed to smile at the couple who entered the store and walked past her, hands linked, talking low and warmly to one another.

See how I don't want that at all? She thought as she took a sheet of bubble wrap and carefully covered the exquisite shepherd with it. Okay, she was just saying that to protect herself. To try to make it true. It was basic psychology. You simply couldn't lose anyone you loved truly, if you refused to love anyone that much.

By the time she'd boxed the figurine, wrapped it and added the purchase to Opal Finch's charge account, Katherine was ringing up the soldier and his wife, who had purchased a blown-glass angel, a last-minute gift.

It took all her strength, but she couldn't stop a great sense of loss from wrapping around her. Wasn't she supposed to be forgetting Mitch? Moving on with her life? She'd prayed and prayed for God to take this love from her heart, but it remained, stubborn and strong no matter what she did to try to get rid of it.

She delivered the gift to Opal, waiting in the reading area where refreshments and Christmas cookies were set out on red-clothed tables. Opal glanced up from chatting with her daughter, and her smile shone warmly. "You are a lifesaver, dear girl. I was at my wit's end when I learned Margie's mother-in-law was coming to town after all."

"I'm glad I could help." Kelly handed the bagged package to Opal's youngest daughter, a lovely middle-aged woman with Opal's same smile and gracious manner. "If there's anything else you need, you just let me know. I hope you both have a Merry Christmas."

"I wish you Merry Christmas, too, dear." Opal looked lovely and content as she sipped from her cup of holiday blend tea. "Margie and I have done all our running for the day, and it's a comfort to sit right here and enjoy the decorations. Will I see you at the candlelight service tonight?"

Kelly fetched the teapot, still hot in its cozy, and removed the insulated cover. She leaned to fill Opal's cup. "I'll be there."

"Wonderful. Why, you'll just have to meet my new great-grandbaby. She's just three weeks old, but good as an angel. You make sure and come find us."

"I promise," she vowed as she filled Margie's cup.

If Kelly was given a wish to be fulfilled by the angels on this cold Christmas Eve night, it would be to have a life like Opal's. To be content in her golden years with family she took joy in, and a life behind her in which each and every day had been filled with love, as would all her days to come. Loving Mitch, of course.

Too bad she wasn't the kind of girl who believed in wishes and dreams.

Although how she wanted to.

"Kelly, did you read from your devotional this

morning?" Opal asked over the rim of her teacup. "'With the Lord, nothing is impossible.'"

Kelly replaced the teapot on the table. How did she answer that? Some thing *were* impossible, she knew that for certain. "I did read the passage."

"I'm holding out hope for you." Opal's eyes twinkled. "It's the season for miracles, you know."

"I know, and there's more to life than studying. I can't argue with that." Mitch. Why did she think of him and miracles in the same breath?

The store's frantic Christmas Eve rush had thinned ten minutes before closing time. As she pitched in to help Katherine catch up on the gift-wrapping at the front counter, she tried to get her thoughts in the right place. No more thinking of Mitch. End of story.

As she folded and taped the last corner of Mr. Brisbane's gift, Katherine surprised her by withdrawing a small package from her blazer pocket, wrapped in simple gold tissue paper. "I know we're exchanging presents when you come over to dinner tomorrow, but I want you to have this. It will look perfect on your Christmas tree."

Kelly studied the small gift that fitted in the palm of her hand. "Thanks, Katherine. Should I open it now?"

"No, this is definitely something you should open alone. Why don't you do that now? Go. I wanted to let you go earlier, paid of course, as a treat, but who knew we were going to be so busy?"

"I have no one waiting for me at home. I can stay and help you close."

"I'm not doing anything but unplugging the coffeepot, counting down the tills and setting the alarm. That's it. So, go on." Katherine took the gift from Kelly's hand, snapped a gift bag open and dropped it in, and clipped around the long counter. "Go home, Kelly. Merry Christmas."

"Merry Christmas, Katherine." She so loved working for the McKaslins. There was no way she would ever feel lonely in her life, not when she had the blessing of truly nice people in it. There was little to do but to wave good-bye to Opal and her daughter, grab her coat and backpack and trudge out the back door.

Snow fell in a thick veil, scouring her as she fought her way to her car. Her poor ten-year-old sedan was buried in snow, and by the time she'd swept off the windows and scraped the crusty layer of ice off the glass, her curiosity was getting the best of her. What had Katherine given her?

Huddled in her cold seat, with the defrosters on high fighting at the foggy windshield, she folded back the tissue paper and there, in a bed of gold, lit by the glow of the dash lights, was a small tin soldier. An ornament for her tree.

Her heart broke into a million pieces, and how could that be? It was already broken. Tears struggled to the surface, no matter how hard she blinked to stop them.

I love him so much, she thought, not knowing if she was wishing or, more, if she were praying. She'd lost too many people she'd loved. That was her life, it was not going to change. It was impossible. Right?

Mitch was an elite soldier. Talk about a risky profession. And it wasn't only the fear of him being killed in combat, but the fact that he belonged in California, and that she was safer with him far away.

This was the path God had made for her, and she clung to it with everything she had. It felt as if the ground was crumbling beneath her feet and she was holding on to a fraying rope. Watching it unravel. Watching it snap.

Knowing she about to fall.

With the Lord, nothing is impossible. The text seemed to follow her as she put her car in gear and navigated through the storm. Or was it the fear in her own heart? She tried to banish memories of the lost little girl she'd been, stubbornly clinging to the hope for the happy endings, like those she read in books.

She fought against the memories as she negotiated the icy city, but the images of Christmases past rose up, unbidden and unwanted. The Christmas Eves her mom had come home horribly drunk or high, and the Christmas Eves when she hadn't come home at all.

As a little girl, Kelly would sit in the living room of whatever apartment they'd been in that year, with no glow from a Christmas tree and no presents, and wish on the brightest star in the sky, which she'd thought was the real Christmas Star, for her mom to get well. For a place to belong. To grow up like the princess in the fairy tales and find true love, a good handsome prince—just like Mitch—and a happily ever after.

Even now, there was Mitch. In her thoughts. In her heart. In her soul. Snow fell harder as she eased down the street in front of her apartment building. If she saw a tan Jeep covered with snow along the curb, it had to be her imagination. She pulled into the nearly vacant lot—most students had fled campus for home—and shut off the car.

Snow tapped in big determined flakes, blanketing her windshield. She glanced at the ornament, cloaked in night shadows, and felt the truth bubble to the surface. She still felt like that little girl, deep at heart, alone in the dark, afraid of being alone forever. The little girl feared she wasn't good enough to love. And if something good happened to her, then it wouldn't last.

Now she was an adult with the same fears, fears she'd never faced, and never overcome. Maybe pushing everything down wasn't the best way to deal with them, she knew, but it didn't matter now.

Tucking her heart away, she zipped the soldier ornament into her backpack and stepped out into the freezing storm. The snow tapped loudly, filling the eerie emptiness of the parking lot. Her thoughts drifted to Mitch, always to Mitch. Where was he on this holy night? Was he cold or warm? In hostile territory or home with his family? He'd come back from his last mission safely, right?

Wherever he was, she wished him warm, safe thoughts. She would always love him, no matter what, no matter how far away and how separate their paths in life.

A hunched shadow emerged from around the corner of the building, barely visible through the haze of snowfall.

Alarm coiled through her even before she recognized the woman's voice, the sound from her past, the sound of her fears.

"K-Kelly, my sweet baby? Is that you?" Her mother's thin hair sticking out beneath a worn-looking knitted hat was gray, and her face was marked by time and hard wear. She had that false look of caring on her face.

Kelly took a step back, fighting down the shame and the hurt roiling up out of the shadows of memories. She caught a faint scent of cheap whiskey. Of course her mom was drinking. She knew her mother would never change, and that meant the woman had come for sympathy and to try to steal something to support her other habits. It was the past that hurt so much, the memories and the betrayal. "You have to go back to the shelter, Mom. It's not that far."

"But I come all this way. In the cold. Just to see my baby girl."

"No, Mom. You know you're supposed to keep away from me." She felt the weight of the past like an open wound, bleeding and raw. "The court says you have to."

"But I'm clean." She swayed as she limped along the snowy walkway. "I brought you a present. Are you gonna let me come in?"

"I don't want something you stole." The rank scent of cheap alcohol on the wind was stronger, bringing up memories that cut straight to her spirit. "I'm sorry. You have to go now. Go back where you belong."

"That is no way to treat your mother. What is wrong with you? No wonder you're all alone. You think you're so high and mighty, but go ahead. All that praying won't change the truth. You're still the same down deep."

She knew that her mom was drunk and mean, but logic didn't rule the heart. Nor did fears nurtured by a lifetime of being alone. Kelly took another step back, whipped her cell phone out of her pocket. "Mom, you aren't supposed to leave the shelter, I'm sure. So, if you'll be nice, I'll call a cab and pay the fare for you. Or I can call the police. It's up to you."

"Why, you no good little—"

Before her mother could fly at her, a tall, powerfully shouldered man materialized soundlessly out of the shadows. Coming through the thickly falling snow and shadows, he caught Dora Logan by the upper arm, subduing her. "You heard Kelly. You need to get to a shelter, or you'll be dealing with the cops."

Mitch. His baritone boomed with authority. He radiated honorable strength. That attractive capable masculinity. Just like that, he was in her life again. Towering before her, looking like her best and brightest wish, too good to be true. Sweet longing welled up through her soul.

As her mother left, sputtering curse words that faded as she melted into the darkness, Mitch remained, invincible, at her side. For an instant, she felt as if it was summer again, with sunshine on her face and Mitch's presence like a steady light in her heart.

But then she realized he had to have heard her mom's words. Every last one of them. The damage was done. Her head hung, and in the endless stretch of silence between her and Mitch, she couldn't think of a single thing to say to make this better, to erase the echo of her mother's words. Or the truth of them.

She heard the icy flakes tap against her hood as she stumbled toward the steps. Her throat was one giant knot of misery she couldn't speak past, not even to thank him. For, in saving her, he'd learned the terrible truth of who she was and where she came from.

He now knew that beneath the responsible girl and straight-A student and faithful Christian, she was afraid that she wasn't worthy of being loved. That her past was like a wandering black hole sucking up all the goodness that would ever happen in her life.

She started up the snow-covered stairs, shame sputtering through her.

"Kelly, are you all right?"

She shook her head; she wasn't all right. His question was like a knife piercing deep. She hesitated midstep. "Thank you for—" She couldn't look him in the eye so she stared into the storm where her mom had disappeared. Her throat closed up again. What did she do now?

"C'mon, let's get you out of the cold." Mitch padded towards her like a lone alpha wolf.

She didn't have to look to know how shadows darkened the hazel-green of his eyes or to see the wince of sorrow around his mouth. She felt the emotion in his heart as if it were her own. She didn't want to feel so much, to be too close to anyone. Ever again.

But he was coming ever closer, the nearly silent sound of his boots halted directly behind her. She could feel his affection radiating like the wind against her cheek, and when she heard the faint rustle of his jacket she knew, even before the solid weight of his big hand settled on the dip of her shoulder. Peace trickled into her cracked heart like hope, like mercy. And her love for him flared brightly, like a light burning despite the darkness, a love she could not put out.

His touch remained, firmly guiding her as they ascended the steps together. Helpless to stop him, unable to speak, her hopes gone, she swiped the snow from her face and felt tears burn behind her eyes. Whatever she did, she would not cry. Could not.

She had to face this—face him—with as much dignity as she could muster. She was a pro when it came to pushing shame and hurt down into the rooms of her heart and locking the door. She had to do that now.

He was going to withdraw now—she knew it. He'd seen her in a different light—and he would never see her the same way again. The only thing she could do was to expect his coming rejection and his inevitable departure.

Her fingers fumbled stupidly with her key ring.

"Let me." His words were a gentle fan against her cheek as he leaned closer and took the keys from her.

For Mitch, all it took was one touch to her hand and a supernova of certainty blazed through him. He felt whole. It felt right, having her here at his side. Tenderness brightened in degree and volume until his heart could not hold it all.

As he unlocked the door and held it for her, blocking the worst of the wind-driven cold, he had time to think. He could see why Kelly was so persistent at pushing him away. Well, other than Joe, whose leaving had been accidental, he could see a long line of people in Kelly's life who hadn't had the character or the inner fiber to love her enough to stick by her.

It made sense, he thought, as he followed her into the apartment and closed the door against the driving snow, that she'd lost faith. She felt her heart had been broken too much. A long line of experiences of never belonging, of never having anyone to depend on, might lead you to believe that.

But he was the one man who knew how to stand and fight for what—and who—mattered. He saw now why people risked so much for the chance at real love. For the chance to make a marriage work, despite the uncertainty and the failure rate. He would have no life of any value unless he had her at his side. She gave meaning to his life. To him.

The question was, had he come all this way for nothing? He couldn't see an answer either way, yes or no, as she shrugged out of her snow-flocked parka.

He was used to danger, he was well-trained and prepared to handle any adversity in the field. He risked his life every time he went out on a mission. He spent his life training and working and practicing to be good at what he did. But when it came to Kelly, he was walking along a vulnerable path. No flak jacket existed to protect him from heartbreak if she shot him down.

She held out her hand for her keys. "Th-thank you for coming along when you did." Her voice echoed faintly in the hallway, and she didn't meet his gaze. "I-I'm glad you're back safely."

"Good." Mitch placed her keys in her gloved palm. "I need to know that you care for me. And how much."

What did she do with this man and his constant caring? She wanted to lash out, to say whatever it took to push him back, to put safe distance between her heart and his.

She squared her shoulders and faced all six-feet-two-inches of him. If only there was a way to change the deepest places within her, all the cracks and old wounds, so that she was good enough and whole enough to try to hold a dream again. A part of her wanted to tell him the truth, the part of her that loved him beyond all reason and good sense and with every last bit of her soul.

He padded closer, soundlessly, as stealthy as a stalking wolf, until he towered over her, close enough to touch, one hundred percent good man and noble heart. "Maybe it would help if I went first."

"I don't think that will help at all." All it would do was to shatter her a little deeper. She had no more strength, she was not strong enough to keep the walls around her soul from crashing down.

He took a box out of his pocket and cradled it in his palm. "This is why I'm here. To ask you to be my wife."

Yes, her heart answered. She knew it was impossible, she was too afraid to believe. Her soul ached with dreams yet to be made and wished and to come true.

Step away, Kelly. Right now. Her heart did not want to. Her soul felt ripped apart and she couldn't do it. She wanted to pray for the chance to say yes to this man, to wear his wedding ring and take his name and share his life.

There I go, dreaming again. Believing in fairy tales. She was a realist these days and not a dreamer. She would keep both feet on the ground. Mitch was not hers to keep. Not now. Not ever.

All the prayers in the world wouldn't change it.

Wait, her heart told her. *Only* prayer can change it.

He cradled her chin with his free hand, gazing down at her and in his hazel eyes she could see his soul, full of love for and devotion to her.

Both the little girl she'd been and the woman she was ached to know what real love was like—real love that could last. That could shelter her from the storms of life, that would show her a loving man's tenderness and care.

If only she could have this man to love. If only God could see fit to change her path, change her destiny and give her this one chance. *Please, Lord.* Her entire soul shattered with need.

As if Mitch heard her prayers, he slanted his mouth over hers. Her spirit stilled. Her heart paused. He covered her lips with his in a tender caress.

Her soul sighed. His kiss was like a dream. Sweetness filled her. Like the river whirling over the rapids, the power of it burst through her with the purest force—and there was no way to stop it. She breathed in the brightness. She curled her fingers into his snow-damp shirt and held on to this perfect moment. Where there was no emptiness. No shadows. No pain.

Just the rush of true love swirling up from her soul. Filling the emptiness. Pushing out the shadows. Healing every crack and fissure and broken place inside.

"I know you're afraid of loving and losing again," he said as he pulled an engagement ring of pearls and diamonds from the box he held. "But I want you to know that the love I have for you in my heart is infinite. Nothing can end it. Nothing can diminish it. Not hardship, not distance and not death. The truth is, only God knows what is going happen, but I want you to know I'm committed. I want to walk the rest of my life with you. So, will you marry me?"

She rubbed the heel of her hand over her heart, surprised it was whole. Didn't the Bible tell her to hold on until morning? All sorrows ended, all hurts would heal, and joy would come? She had enough faith, after all, to dream. "I love you with all of my soul. Yes, I will marry you."

"I am so glad." He slipped the ring on her trembling finger. "Because my mother is hoping you'll come to church with us tonight. She's vowed to spoil you. As for me," he brought her into his arms and cradled her to his heart, "I'm going to love you forever."

"That's a promise I'm going to make you keep." She saw the future stretch out before her, full of promise, of family, of loving Mitch.

It was a night of miracles, she thought, as she laid her cheek against his granite chest. It had been a rough journey, but God had seen her through. He had brought her here, to Mitch. She was sure now that there would be more miracles to come.

* * * * *

Don't miss Jillian Hart's next
inspirational romance in
her Christmas short story
"CHRISTMAS, DON'T BE LATE"
in the Steeple Hill collection
A MERRY LITTLE CHRISTMAS,
available November 2006.

Dear Reader,

Thank you for choosing *A Soldier for Christmas*. I hope you enjoyed Kelly's story as much as I did writing it. Kelly fears her past may always have a hold on her and that's why she's afraid to believe in the possibility of a happy future. That is until the right man comes along to show her differently.

Sometimes it is so hard to understand why we have to go through difficulties or pain in our lives. It is a comfort to know that God doesn't leave us to deal with hard times alone, but walks with us through our sorrow to the other side, where joy is always waiting. If you are walking through a painful time, please don't lose hope. The best is yet to come.

Wishing you peace and grace,

Jillian Hart

QUESTIONS FOR DISCUSSION

1. How important has Kelly's faith been in helping her out of a difficult past? In what ways?

2. What is the importance of the theme of service to others in *A Soldier for Christmas?*

3. What impact does prayer have on the developing love story?

4. Kelly learns that God has led her to a place of hope. Have you faced this experience in your life?

5. Kelly and Mitch have similar values. How important is this to their developing relationship?

6. Kelly and Mitch have vastly different experiences in life. How does this stand in the way of their romance? How does it help? How do these experiences make them stronger?

7. Kelly is afraid to open her heart to love. How does Mitch manage to get beneath Kelly's defenses?

8. How does falling in love with Mitch change Kelly forever? How does falling in love with Kelly change Mitch, even half a world away?

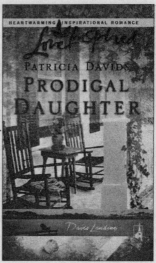

WITH CHRISTMAS IN HIS HEART

BY

GAIL GAYMER MARTIN

Her plan was to come to Mackinac Island to care for her ailing grandmother—not to fall in love. Meeting her grandmother's enigmatic boarder, Will Lambert, made Christine Powers rethink her workaholic ways. But when her boss demanded she return, could she leave Will behind?

Available November 2006 wherever you buy books.

Steeple
Hill®

LIWCIHH

www.SteepleHill.com

REQUEST YOUR FREE BOOKS!

2 FREE INSPIRATIONAL NOVELS
PLUS 2
FREE
MYSTERY GIFTS

YES! Please send me 2 FREE Love Inspired® novels and my 2 FREE mystery gifts. After receiving them, if I don't wish to receive any more books, I can return the shipping statement marked "cancel." If I don't cancel, I will receive 4 brand-new novels every month and be billed just $3.99 per book in the U.S., or $4.74 per book in Canada, plus 25¢ shipping and handling per book and applicable taxes, if any*. That's a savings of at least 20% off the cover price! I understand that accepting the 2 free books and gifts places me under no obligation to buy anything. I can always return a shipment and cancel at any time. Even if I never buy another book from Steeple Hill, the two free books and gifts are mine to keep forever.

113 IDN EF26   313 IDN EF27

Name	(PLEASE PRINT)	
Address		Apt.
City	State/Prov.	Zip/Postal Code

Signature (if under 18, a parent or guardian must sign)

Order online at www.LoveInspiredBooks.com

Or mail to Steeple Hill Reader Service™:

IN U.S.A.	IN CANADA
P.O. Box 1867	P.O. Box 609
Buffalo, NY	Fort Erie, Ontario
14240-1867	L2A 5X3

Not valid to current Love Inspired subscribers.

Want to try two free books from another series?
Call 1-800-873-8635 or visit www.morefreebooks.com